PSYCHO CHICK AND HER GOD

MARILYN STRONG

Published by Firebaptized Publishing
Printed in USA

TABLE OF CONTENTS

DRAFT

To my parents Sarah and Leroy Strong, Sr.

DRAFT

REROUTING THE TRAFFIC

There was a cool breeze coming through my car windows as I drove home from the grocery store. I delighted in the smell of a fresh cut lawn on this lovely Thursday evening. I was cruising down Grand River Street in my Silver Ford Lincoln. I turned up the radio; my favorite song was playing.

I lean a little to the right. I threw my left wrist over the steering wheel and let my hand drop, and then I pop my fingers to the song.

"Sing that song Sam, with your fine self."

The rear view mirror was bouncing to the bass. My head was bobbing up and down to the beat. My hair looked like a famous female entertainer when the fan is blowing during a concert.

Traffic was backed up as a result of an accident on the Southfield Freeway.

The detour took the traffic off of Grand River through the Rosedale Park community.

"This takes me past my man James' house."

I slowed down to see if he was sitting on the porch.

"Oh naw, to the naw, I know I don't see that green Ford Escape in his driveway parked next to his white Chrysler 300."

I circled the block again to make sure I'm looking at the right house.

"Who does he think he was messing with? We just talked about this female yesterday."

I parked in the driveway, blocking in her vehicle. The curtains were drawn and he didn't know I was outside.

I tried to calm myself and prepare for a rational conversation. My blood was boiling and my stomach was quivering.

I called James' home phone; it went straight to voice mail. "This man was pissing me off."

I called his cell phone.

"Hello"

"Hello back at you. What are you doing?"

"I can't talk right now, let me call you back."

"No baby; I know what's going on inside your house. You will talk to me right now."

He hangs up the phone.

I keep my gun with me. In these streets, I would rather the cops catch me with it than Pookie and Ray Ray catch me without it. I reached into the glove box and pulled out my gorgeous mother of pearl handle Hogue gun with Red Laser Grips.

I pointed it at her vehicle. The laser locked on the windshield; "Rat-a-tat-tat." I heard the shells hit the ground. The smoke went in my nostrils and I choked.

It was such a sight to see her windshield full of holes then shatter.

I was on autopilot.

Now his car. Rat-a-tat-tat-tat.

"The headlights and windshield are full of holes."

I stepped behind my car in the middle of the street and yelled.

"Come out of the house now and talk to me, you one testicle limp noodle."

James ran out shirtless, showing his six pack. His chest had toned muscles I had not noticed. He had on the pajama pants I bought, and he was hauling butt barefoot.

"Elizabeth, what are you doing? You crazy, witch?" He screamed from the top stair. He was pointing and cussing as he was walking down the stairs.

The sight of him, made the rage reach the boiling point. The more I looked at him, the more distraught I became. I felt like a robot. I can't believe his whore came out of the house and was standing on the porch behind him. This pissed me off more. I snapped. I felt a rush and could not control whatever possessed me.

Just as he reached the bottom step, I locked the laser on his chest, and open fired. I felt the kick back. I got off two rounds before he was spread eagle on the sidewalk.

I heard the shells hit the ground again. The smell of the smoke lodged in my throat and started coughing.

His whore was in plain view now, looks like she has a new wig. She was trying to run back in the house.

"OK, witch, it is on, now take this."

I pointed at her new wig on her big head, squeezed the trigger but I missed.

She was frantically trying to open the front door. Quickly, I locked on her back; I missed and shot her in the leg. I squeezed off two rounds. I thought I missed, but she fell.

I did my happy dance. This is revenge to the infinite degree.

"Bang, Bang the witch is dead, the wicked witch is dead."

I threw my hands up in a football field goal victory.

There was an eerie silence for about 30 seconds then the police sirens and lights flooded the street. My rational mind kicked in. "OK, this is not good. It is time to think. I can't run because the cops will hunt me down like a dog. I have to be submissive to them.

I'm not trying to die an unlawful death like Ms. **Anderson in Ohio who was killed by the law enforcement while they tried to restrain her.** Or like **Ms. Smith when nervous police shot her in Texas as she walked up to them."**

I placed my gun on the ground and stepped away. I sat on the curb waiting for them to put on the bracelets.

"Miss, did you see what happened?" The cop said walking toward me with his gun drawn.

"Yes, I did." I said with a slow nod.

"Will you quickly enlighten us?"

"Actually, I shot them both."

"What?"

I held out my wrists and did not resist. In one sweep he hit me on the back of my head and knocked me on the ground. I was face down with a nosebleed.

He shouted. "Spread them, witch."

"Oh, my God, you are hurting me. Stop it; you are going to break my shoulder bones bending them back. Police Brutality. I hope someone is recording this." I said to the crowd that was gathering.

He cuffed me behind my back and yanked me up. He was dragging me to the police car while the crowd was taking pictures. He didn't try to protect my head he just threw me in the back seat. I position my head making the blood from my nose dripped on their car seat and not on my clothes.

I looked out the window.

There were a couple of EMS vehicles, taking away the one testicle and his whore. More cop cars than I could count.

Jail life was no joke. I was given one phone call. All of my numbers were in my cell phone. The only number I remembered was to the church. I left a message for the secretary to call my brother. I was scared of jail based on the stuff you see on TV. I didn't want to meet a "salad tossing" chick. There were four beds in a cell and one toilet. Most of the women hook up in the showers. Contrary to what's on TV, you never ask "What are you in for?" They can ask you, but it's a fight if you ask them. I always looked straight ahead while walking. I stayed in my cell most of the time.

Rerouting the traffic on Grand River also rerouted the traffic flow of my life.

THE YOUNG PSYCHO CHICK

I was seven years old when my mother's boyfriend got in the bed with me.

"Mamma I am scared, come and help me." I cried.

He put one hand over my mouth and the other between my legs. He put his immense fingers into me and he was moaning and kissing my neck. He reeked of cigarettes and beer. His breath was like decaying garbage in the alley.

He started moving his fingers real hard and fast, up and down and sideways. It hurt a lot. Then he took my hand and forced it between his legs and started moving my hand up and down. I didn't know what to do when mamma didn't come.

I let the tears fall without a sound. I was as quiet as a mouse while silently praying to God to make him stop. It seemed like it lasted for hours. The next day, I told Mamma.

"Stop lying little girl. He would never do that."

Then, he walked into the kitchen.

"Peter, did you get in bed with this girl last night?"

"Honey, I must admit she was an exquisite sweet little chocolate drop. But no baby, I didn't touch her. But, I've seen the type; she is fast and will probably get pregnant in a few years, you better watch her."

When he left for work, Momma took a puff from her funny smelling cigarette and snatched me up by my collar.

"Little girl, are you trying to be grown. I know you are trying to seduce my man. I've seen you walking around here flirting with him.

Peter is good to me, and I can't afford to let him go because you are discovering you can do more with it than piss."

She dragged me to my bedroom, threw me on the mattress face down and tied my hands and feet to the bed frame and walked out of the room. After some time had passed, I decided to call for her.

"Mamma I am sorry. I promise I won't do anything wrong again. I want to get up now. I need to use the bathroom and Mamma I am hungry too." I called.

After several hours, she came back into the room. Without saying a word, she started hitting me across my back with the extension cord. I screamed and yelled, but I could not break free. I counted the licks. She hit me 20 times. I could feel the blood running through my clothes and onto the mattress. After I wet the bed, she stopped.

"I am sending you to live with your Uncle and Aunt across town. I can't stand the sight of your ugly face." She said in an exhausted voice.

I never saw my mamma after that, and I never knew my real father.

My aunt and uncle adopted me. They had a son named Jacob. My new dad was kind and gentle and never came into my bedroom.

My brother always pulls my hair.

"Stop it Jacob that hurts."

"Is Madison mad? Mad-mad Madison." He teased me.

It made me furious when he said mad-mad Madison.

"I'm goanna tell mom if you don't stop."

"You better not tell or I will beat you up, mad-mad Madison."

He thought he was the boss of me because he was the oldest.

I finally got the courage to tell mom.

"Mom, Jacob keeps pulling my hair and it hurts."

"Don't be a tattletale. He is your brother, and you should love him and try to get along. I'm sure it does not hurt that much."

"So is it alright for him to hurt me and nothing happens to him?"

"Don't you talk back to me, little missy."

"Yes Ma'am."

I put my head down and walked away. I felt unprotected and unloved.

I went to my dad.

"Dad, Jacob keeps pulling my hair." I said as I stood next to him while he was watching the football game.

"Boy." He calls for Jacob. "Why are you pulling your sister's hair?"

"No Dad, I didn't do it. I don't know why she is saying that."

"Leave her alone. You kids get somewhere and sit down."

"Thank you Dad."

The hair pulling got worse, and I got headaches. I dare not tell Dad again. I don't know what Jacob will do to me.

Each night I pray and ask God "Why does he do this when I didn't do anything to him?"

Since I could not fight my brother and win, I got revenge for the headaches.

I threw away box cars from his beloved Polar Express Lionel Train Set. I bent train tracks in his spare parts box.

DRAFT

SCHOOL LESSONS

I valued going to school and learning. At the Academy my teachers were nice. They looked like they were in a Fashion Magazine. I wanted to be a teacher when I grew up.

This day I was dressed in my uniform. My hair was freshly braided. I felt cute, confident and ready for the world.

"Hey Jacob, hey there." I try to flag him down to say hi.

Jacob turned around with an indignant look on his face and pushed me against the locker.

"Don't ever speak to me when I am with my friends."

"Why not?"

He looked very angry.

"Ok, I won't." I was embarrassed and surprised at his reaction. It seemed like the entire school saw what he did.

The next day, I saw Jacob in the hall and he passed me like we didn't know each other. I felt invisible and irrelevant like I didn't matter.

I turned the corner and was a few steps away from my classroom, when I ran into the school bully, Donald. He was light-skinned and was the only black person and I knew with red hair and freckles. His shirt was seldom tucked in his pants. His huge belly was showing. His gym shoes are dirty run over. They say he lived in a shelter.

When I saw Donald, my heart dropped into my stomach. I heard the Jaws theme music "Jun, jun, jun, jun". He walked up to me and without saying a word punched me in the stomach.

I bent over and then he pulled my hair to show my face; I dropped my books and papers.

"No, No, stop. Stop It Donald." I screamed louder.

He slapped me and pushed me down.

"You ugly black girl, no one likes you."

I was sobbing and curled up in a corner, too scared to fight back. No one helped me. The whole school was standing around laughing. I could not find a familiar face in the crowd. I was just waiting for him to stomp me with those run over shoes.

Out of the blue, Jacob appeared running around the corner looking like a superhero mix. My big brother had the speed of the Black Panther the strength of Superman and the power of the Hulk.

His uniform shirt was unbuttoned, and waiving in the air, like a cape. His friends were running behind him. It looked like they were moving in slow motion and fast-forward at the same time. I hoped he was coming to help me, and not to be friends with Donald.

"I got this baby girl." Jacob whispered in my ear as he leaned over and smiled. I stood up and the pain in my stomach stopped.

My big brother kicked Donald's butt. He punched him in the face and stomach. Dust and papers were flying everywhere. Then Jacob body slammed Donald.

"Oh, Snap" the crowd yelled.

"Get him Jacob, get him." I cheered him on.

When Jacob let him go, Donald sat on the floor against the lockers with a bloody nose, torn shirt and a bruised ego.

"Don't ever touch my sister again, or I will kill you!" Jacob told him as he pointed his finger at Donald's face.

My big brother gathered my books and papers, put his arm around my shoulders and walked me to my class. After school, he walked home with me and not his friends. I felt validated. The hair pulling stopped, but I still could not talk to him when he was with his friends unless he spoke first. He said it was a guy thing.

DRAFT

TROUBLESOME TEEN LESSONS

I could not comprehend why we had to go to church so much. Monday youth meeting, Tuesday Adult Choir rehearsal, Wednesday bible study, Thursday youth choir rehearsal, and Friday was youth department day.

I enjoyed Friday the most. Only teens were allowed, and we had one adult supervisor, Mr. Kelly. He was cool. He would bring Coke-a-cola and potato chips. He called it coke and chip hour.

One Friday, one of the older guys brought peanuts. "Put these peanuts in your coke." He said.

I liked him. He always dressed well and was nice to me. Later he taught me how to hot-wire a car. He was known on the streets as ruthless. I heard he shot and killed someone. But he was kind to me.

Mr. Kelly wrote a play, and we were having play rehearsal. While enjoying my coke, chips and peanuts, two guys started fighting. Mr. Kelly sprang into action.

"What are you guys doing? If you want to fight, do it and get paid for it." He brought out boxing gloves and taught them how to box. I watched intensely, just in case I ran into Donald I would be ready. One of the guys later won a Golden Gloves Award for boxing.

My mom thought it would be a good idea to take Kenpo classes. I competed in a couple of tournaments and earned a few belts. Each week I walked out of the *Dojo* (Training house) wanting someone to mess with me. "I was pumped, now bring it on."

One Friday after Coke and Chip hour, Jacob and I had a heart to heart talk.

"I am going to King High School and you will stay at East English Village High school. I won't be able to protect you anymore."

"That's OK Jacob. I will be fine."

"I'm sure you will be."

I thought this would be an opportune time to ask him a question I have been pondering.

"Jacob, when I was younger, why did you always pull my hair?"

"Because I could, that's what boys do when we want to control girls."

"Are you kidding me; that is stupid."

"You see baby girl, I knew you were smarter than me, and you could get your way with Dad. I had to do something to make you feel deflated and bring you down because I didn't like myself when I compared myself to you. When I pulled your hair, it made me feel powerful because you were hurting too and I controlled how you felt. Did you follow my warped logic? I am sorry I was mean to you."

"Yes, I follow your logic. Apology accepted. I'm sorry I threw away some of your train parts."

"You did what?"

"Yep, I only threw them away when I got headaches from you pulling my hair. Your train collection was the only way I could fight you."

Jacob let out a belly laugh.

"I wondered what happened to those box cars and tracks. Apology accepted, I guess I deserved it."

"Yes, you did. I love you Jacob."

"I love you more Madison."

We embraced.

I was ready for my first day of High school. Finally, I don't have to wear a uniform. I was dressed in a beautiful red blouse and designer jeans designed that were a snug fit. My hair was whipped, and my shoes were imitation "red bottom." I had one book in my arms and the others in a knock off designer backpack.

I remember what my dad told me. "Always walk in a room like you own it the Mother."

I was hearing my dad's voice as I walk with confidence while looking for my classroom. I was not paying attention to all of the noise and students.

East English High school was tough; a hand full of white students, more Hispanic and half the school are African American students.

I run into Donald as I turn the corner to my classroom. This fool was dressed in torn jeans and a white "wife beater" t-shirt. He looks like a reject from Happy Days.

I heard the music from Jaws. My heart was beating hard and wild, I know he heard it. I wish my superhero brother was in the building.

I stood with my shoulders square and stared him in the eyes, ready to do battle.

"How are you today?" He said as he was walking toward me, with his hand extended to shake.

"I'm fine, what's up with you?"

"Listen, Madison, we are older, and I don't want any trouble, let's call it a truce."

I shook his hand.

"Can I get a hug?"

"OK, since we are calling it a truce."

We had a quick, awkward hug.

"Thank you Madison, this means a lot to me."

"No problem, see you around."

Maybe I've gained a friend. Or the martial arts training and confidence stuff scared him.

The second day of school, my friend met me in the hall before my first class.

"Donald was going around the school calling you a slut and said he had sex with you over the summer."

"What, it is not true. How can he say that and people believe him?"

"Madison, I saw you hugging him yesterday; I believe you slept with him. See you around girl, I can't hang out with you anymore; you know what they say; birds of a feather flock together." Then she ran to her class.

I could feel myself getting heated. I had to calm myself down and think. When I got home, I checked all social media avenues. It was everywhere.

My face plastered on someone's body, with him on top. I thought I would die of shame.

The next day, I found him in the hall walking with his friends and confronted him.

"Donald, why are you doing this? You know it's not true."

"I don't like you because you think you are all that. Besides I was bored and needed something to do."

I could feel mad-mad Madison coming out.

"What? This is unfair; you are ruining my reputation for something I didn't do. Take it down, or I will tell my brother."

"I ain't scared of your brother, he's in another school anyway and you can't do anything to me".

Donald made an ugly face and then he and his friends laughed at me.

I never felt so irritated. I started to get warm, my hands were sweating and then I felt fire slowly crawling up my back, swirling around in my head; it felt like Jacob was pulling my hair out of my head. Then I snapped. Here comes mad-mad Madison.

I let out a yell and executed a back fist punch to his nose. I heard the bone snap. As he was going down backwards I screamed and caught him with a front snap kick to the shin and I broke his right leg. Then I took the heel of my designer shoe and stomped on his left foot. I was pretty sure I broke a bone.

He was crying like a little girl. I felt empowered by the revenge. I was gloating inside. "This Tae Kwon Do stuff really works."

"Donald got beat up by a girl." His friends were teasing him. They scattered like roaches when the hall monitors arrive.

The teachers were running like there was a fire. Little girl Donald was sobbing and crying. Snot mixed with the blood from his nose was rolling down his fat face. I felt no pity for him. Ice water was running through my veins.

"Young lady, what have you done?" One of the teachers asked as she looked surprised.

I had to think swiftly. "I defended myself. He was trying to fight me. I didn't have a choice. He was going to beat me up."

"No she is lying, I didn't do anything." Little girl Donald responded.

They believed him. I was expelled and he went to the hospital. The next day, the social media posts were taken down.

Mom and dad didn't play when it came to school.

"Why are you fighting in school?" Mom said.

I got flash backs from when I was younger and got in trouble mom would say "Go outside and get a switch from the tree."

"This was stupid, why do I have to find the thing that was going to hurt me."

"What did you say?"

"Nothing."

"I thought so."

Mom was the typical black mother. She would rhythmically talk while she was swatting my butt with the switch. Black mothers were the first to rap to the beat, not the hip-hop community.

"Didn't I tell you (swat) not to (swat) act up (swat). Now (swat) you are going (swat) to do what I said (swat) and learn and stay out of trouble (swat)."

"Madison Elizabeth, answer me. Why are you fighting at school?" Mom said with a raised voice.

Wow, my whole name means urgency.

I told her the truth in great detail.

"OK, I understand, but you should have let the adults take care of it. Now we have to figure out what to do with you for a week. I will tell your father. Get ready to hear from him."

I thought I blew my privilege to go to the sweetheart dance with Noah at church. I asked if I could still go, surprisingly she said yes.

I could not wait to tell Jacob about the dance. "Noah likes me. I am going to the sweetheart dance with him tonight."

"He's cool."

I was glad Jacob approved of him.

The dance was magical. I had an enchanted time and Noah was the perfect gentleman. He did everything Dad said a guy should do on a date. It felt nice when he held me and we slow danced; it was like he was claiming me. He pulled me close. I felt his penis jump. It scared me and I pulled away. He looked at me and smiled. No words were exchanged. I was glad the slow dance was over.

Noah and I talked on the phone for hours almost every day. I never brought up the slow dance. We would wave to each other at church. No one knew we liked each other. We planned to go to a birthday party next month.

He didn't call three days in a row. I called him. He didn't answer. He avoided me at church. I didn't know what was going on. The day before the birthday party he called.

"Hello."

"Hi Madison, its Noah."

"Yes, I recognize your voice, what's going on, why haven't you called me?"

"I'm calling you now. Do you are still going to the party tomorrow?"

"Yes, I still want to go."

"I will pick you up at 8:00."

"Alright, I will be ready."

The day of the party, he called at 6:00.

"Hello Madison, be ready at 8:00."

"I said I would be ready, don't you be late."

The phone rings at 7:30. "Madison, I might be a little late, but I will be there."

"Noah, how late are you going to be?"

"Oh, a few more minutes. I'm on my way."

"OK" I said in a slightly aggravated tone.

At 8:30 he calls again. "Madison, I'm sorry, don't give up on me, I'm on my way."

"You're only 30 minutes late." I said trying to be understanding of his apparent problem.

At 9:00 he calls again. "Madison, I hope you are ready because I'm almost there."

I was annoyed. "Would you stop calling and get here, we've already missed a lot of the party."

Noah didn't call again and didn't show up. I was heartbroken. Why was he playing this game if he knew he was not going to take me? I cried all night. What did I do to make him treat me like this?

The next morning at breakfast I talked to Jacob.

"I was stood up yesterday by Noah, we were supposed to go to the birthday party and he didn't show up."

"He was a stupid jerk; he does not know how to treat you. He is not worthy of you."

"Jacob, why did he keep calling and saying he was on his way knowing he was not coming?"

"Don't tell me he used the oldest trick in the book? He wanted to make sure you stayed home while he was out with someone else."

"What? Is that something all guys do?"

"Yes, baby girl. I was at the party last night and Noah showed up with some girl who goes to Cass Tech High School. I didn't know he was supposed to bring you or I would have checked him."

"I feel like such a fool." I said and started to cry.

"Please don't cry Madison. Do you want me to take care of him? I don't like him anyway."

"No, don't do that."

"You know Madison; he actually did you a favor. All he wanted to do was to get in your pants. The goal of every boy is to get in those pants. After the Sweetheart dance, he figured out you were not that type of girl. He didn't know how to tell you, so he did this stupid thing hoping you would not like him anymore."

"Good ridden," I said with a smile a fist bump to Jacob.

"Oh heck yes. Good ridden."

"OK Maddie, this is how you play the game. He is dead to you; he does not exist. Do not accept his phone calls. When you see him at church or at school, walk past him, and look beyond him like you don't see him. Do not initiate a hello, a wave or eye contact. Above all, do not flash your traffic-stopping smile." Jacob said with a double fist bump.

"Got it, big brother."

We embraced, and I felt like my old self again. Lesson learned from Noah, remember this phone call trick and don't fall for it again.

LESSONS AS A TEEN

Jacob had a friend named Andrew. Sometimes, I rode with them to church; they made me sit in the back seat so they could holla at the girls. Andrew and I became boyfriend and girlfriend. We would argue a lot.

"Andrew, why don't you call me like you used to?"

"I'm busy with my singing group. Everyone was going crazy; we are going to hit it big soon."

"It only takes one minute to call just to say hi."

"Sorry, I was always moving at a rapid pace. I guess I forgot. Now, do you want to watch a movie or what?"

"Don't try to shut me up. I want to talk about this. I just want to spend some time with you."

"Girl, you are getting on my nerves, just tell me what you want."

"I just did. I want more time with you. Why can't I go when your group sings?"

"Because I never know when we are going, we just get a phone call and we are gone."

I run important issues past my best friend Tee. Her real name was Terri. Her twin was Sherri. Some can't tell them apart. Tee and I have been close friends since I was 5 years old. She was my ride or die friend; my voice of reason, my rock, AKA my person.

Since Tee was a couple of years older, she knew stuff. Sherri and Terri are stylish girls, a little overweight; their skin color looks like milk chocolate. They have died cherry blond hair that is shaved on one side and long on the other. They have the biggest most stunning almond-shaped brown eyes that can look into your soul. Tee's left eye droops a little which was how I tell them apart. Her house always smells like Jasmine.

"Tee I don't know how to make him pay more attention to me. I think he's losing interest."

"Girl give him an ultimatum if he does not listen, kick him to the curb. He should know how to treat you. If he is for you, he will step up. If he is not for you, then the break up was going to happen anyway. Sometimes men need a little reminder of how good you are for and to them."

Filled with the wisdom and knowledge from my best friend, I approached Andrew.

"I am a priority just like your singing group. Show me some respect and plan activities to spend time with me. You have to shape up, or ship out."

To my surprise, he said "I'm going to ship out."

I'm thinking "What just happened here. What went wrong?"

I called Tee sobbing, "He broke up with me."

"Girlfriend, I am sorry it happened."

We had a heart-to-heart talk for about an hour.

About a week later Tee called just to talk. "I have some news for you."

"Ok talk."

"I am pregnant."

"Wow, I didn't know you were dating or sexually active you're only 17."

"How far along are you?"

"Oh, about 2 months."

"Congratulations to you and the father. Girl, you never talk about your boyfriend, who is the father?"

"It's Andrew and we are getting married next month."

"What? Slow down. Are you talking about my Andrew?" I asked, as my stomach drop to the floor.

"Yes girl, I am sorry, it just happened."

"How could it just happen, you are my friend? I trusted you. How could you do this to me?" I hung up the phone and felt like I was going to throw up. I was enraged, I paced in my room. I tore up the picture we took on the roller coaster. Since I was home alone, I screamed until my throat was sore.

"How could they betray me, my best friend and dog of a boyfriend?"

Lesson learned: never trust anyone with all of the information on my relationship, especially a female. Some females are wicked individuals.

Karma is the great equalizer. I found out the dog was beating Tee on a regular basis. They got divorced and she had to move away for her safety. Sherri was lost without Tee. She got on drugs and they found her body in a car in the church parking lot.

The dog married a girl from the church named Myrtle. He openly cheats on Myrtle and flaunts his affair of five years with this ugly woman named Becky (with the bad hair). Becky was his cash cow; she buys him clothes. They take out of town trips together. She even put the down payment on his new Lincoln. She was at all of their family functions.

Myrtle has medical issues and knows Becky was screwing her husband. She believes she can't support herself and her three kids if she leaves him. I felt sorry for her, it was sad.

THE WARDEN OF THE GARDEN OF EDEN

While taking Tempo, I met Samuel who was a black belt master. We clicked. We went out a few times for dinner and a movie.

One day we went out and I was wearing a cute peach knit blouse that buttons in the back. It was fitted around the waist. Since I gained a pound or two, I put on my body shaper. I wore denim hills that perfectly match my jeans and denim earrings. I flat ironed my hair, and it was flowing around my shoulders.

After the movie, we stopped at the Dairy Queen and ate our ice cream in the car at the Park. It was romantic holding hands as we walk through the park.

Today he was trying to rub and touch me too much. I had to check him after he tried to squeeze my butt.

"Samuel, don't do that, we are not at that point in our relationship."

"When will we be at that point? Come on; my body needs you, I can't continue to see you and not have you."

"No, I'm not ready."

He put his hands on my shoulders and shook me hard. "You are a tease; you know you want to do it."

"Get your hands off of me. I said no. Take me home." I raised my voice, "NOW!"

He removed his hands. I didn't want him to know I was past scared. I know I could not fight him and win, and I didn't want to walk home.

"Why do you dress pretty and show your shape, you are just asking for it."

"I can wear whatever I want and it does not give you a license to determine I want sex."

His eyes got as large as saucers and it looked like he was slobbering as he talked. "You listen to me you witch, I have taken you out three times, spent my money on you and now it's time for you to pay the piper. It's time for payback."

"First of all, don't you eve---r call me out of my name again. And secondly, pay you back, pay you back? You are out of your mind. I read a book that said I am the prize. Taking me out was your way of trying to win me, the prize.

"Screw that book." He said.

"Listen; if you don't take me home right now, I will call the cops and even worse, I will tell my father and my brother. They will deal with you."

He pushed me down on the freezing ground, pent my arms down with his knees. I let out a blood-curdling scream.

He tried to tear my blouse, but the knit fabric wouldn't budge. He pulled down my pants.

I was swarming like a snake trying to get free. He put his clammy hands between my stomach and my underwear and started to tug. Thank God for the body shaper. (The warden of the Garden of Eden). It takes skill to put them on and take them off.

"What is this?" He was shocked he could not pull them down.

"Stop it, stop it." I screamed again.

I felt a sting from the hard slap to my face. It really hurt. This pissed me off. I managed to swing my legs up and hit him in back of his head. He loosened his grip setting my arms are free. I took both thumbs and gorged his eyeballs. I tried to pull them out. He screamed then rolled over off of me. I got up, pull up my pants then sprinted toward the street.

It was quiet; I didn't hear him running after me, or a car behind me. The only thing I heard was my breathing and my heart beating rapidly. I was hoping he did not pop up behind me like a classic scene in a horror movie.

I flagged down a taxi. Lucky for me it was one of the guys who attend my church.

"Hey Madison, what you doing out here?"

"I was ready to go and my friends were not, then I decided to catch a cab."

"Un Hu. I'm not buying it, but if that's your story, you can stick to it. What happened to your face?"

"Nothing, I think I had an allergic reaction to some seafood."

"Un Hu. Do you want me to take you home to your mom?"

"Yes, please. Thank you."

The conversation ended, and it took all of my willpower not to cry in the taxi. The fare was $15.00. I am glad I listened to my dad when he said; always keep cash on you, in case of an emergency.

I was too embarrassed to tell my brother or my dad. I applied makeup, wore sunglasses and stayed in my room for a few of days.

Samuel stopped coming to the Dojo. After a few years, I heard he got married. Karma strikes again. He beat his wife until she was unrecognizable and her father pressed charges and he went to jail for 5 years.

Lessons learned – Wear a tight-fitting body shaper, it will keep the Garden of Eden safe. And always keep cash on hand.

DRAFT

LESSONS LEARNED IN THE 20'S

I have always dated cute guys. I made a vow; the next man I date will be ugly, and maybe we will have a fighting chance.

I met Richard in the parking lot after a play at the Music Hall. He was a tall blue-black man. He was blind in one eye. His hair looked like he used a wide-tooth comb to get through that thick afro. His nice slender body made him handsome in his suits. I got a strong vibe from him. He was genuinely a nice guy.

Our relationship worked well for about 3 years. He was at my house more than he is at his. I noticed a young chick named Cathy kept hanging around him. She had the face of a pug dog. I thought someone smashed in her nose, but as it turns out those were her God-given features. Ms. Pug nose would not go away.

"Honey, what's up with Cathy, why is she always in your face?"

"She is just a young girl I'm helping out."

In the pit of my belly, it just didn't feel right.

I approached Pug nose. "Hi there Cathy, I notice you are quite fond of Richard."

"Oh yes, he's like my big brother."

"In that case, consider me your big sister and you can talk to me as much as you talk to Richard. I know you have my phone number, and I have yours because I've seen it on my home phone records."

"OK Ms. Madison I will do that, thank you."

Richard's car was in for repairs, as usual. This presented the perfect opportunity to execute my plan.

I dressed well for work because I had to chair a meeting to demonstrate a new operating system in a morning meeting. I wore a navy blue and white pent stripe skirt suit, with a white blouse; Navy hills and Hanes nylons for the polished look. I sprayed on my favorite perfume. Dad said look good, smell good and do good.

I picked him up and let him drop me off at work so he could use my car to look for another job.

We had a casual conversation on the drive to work.

"I hear the weather is going to be nice today." he said.

"Yep, any day without snow is a good day."

"Ok honey, have a successful meeting and a great day."

"I will, and you have a successful day job hunting babe."

We kiss, and I walked into the office.

The presentation went well. I took the afternoon off. I called my friend Deborah. "Come on girl, we have to do a drive by. I need you and your car."

Deborah was a tall, attractive dark sister with short salt and pepper natural hair. She works out and has an excellent shape. Her makeup was always applied like she was an artist. This girl loves those huge hoop earrings. Once I asked her "are those bracelets or earrings?"

She was street smart but comes across quiet and nonchalant until you step out of line.

Deborah rolls up in her Black on Black Ford Taurus. It was shining like new money.

"What's up girl?" she says.

"I think Richard is hoeing around with this chick name Cathy. We are going to drive by his house."

"Nothing but a word."

We are driving down Puritan, and what do I see, Pug nose Cathy in my car, and she was rubbing his Richard's neck as he drives. My heart started beating quickly, and my hands started to sweat.

"Oh no, follow them Deb."

"We are like the TV show Cheaters."

We laugh.

"Richard does not know your car, so we can follow close. Don't lose them girl."

They stop at the Soul Food Restaurant on Fenkell. When they got out, we got out.

"Hey baby, what's going on here?" I said

Deborah was standing behind me close to the car.

"Hi honey, I was just taking Cathy to lunch."

"Oh really, in my car. You are supposed to be out looking for a job. You don't even take me to lunch." I said while staring down Pug nose.

I raised my voice "Do you think I am stuck on stupid? I should kick your butt and make you say thank you."

I felt myself about to lose control; I had to slow down.

"What you better do is give me my keys and you and this little whore can go back to wherever you came from on foot."

"No Madison, I will not give you the keys. You and Deborah should just keep it moving."

I was surprised at his response, and my head turned around like the young girl in the Exorcist. "What do you mean, NO?"

I felt an uncontrollable rage; boiling blood slowly moving up my back, to my neck and reaching my head. I lost my mind. I heard a voice saying "Don't let him get away with treating you like dirt." Mad-mad Madison came out.

I gave him a right elbow to his rib. When he bent over, I got him with a right hook and a left jab. "Stand up and be a man." I said just to piss him off.

I gave him an uppercut to the chin. Then I grabbed him by the throat. I was going to rip out his Adam's apple, but when he began to fall, I let go and allowed him fall to the ground.

"Give me my keys!"

"No" he shouted, trying to show off in front of Pug Nose.

He tried to reach for my leg to pull me down. It irritated me because he was trying to fight back.

I stomped his thigh with my heel when he was on the ground.

"Richard, I was faithful and helpful to you and you do this to me."

Cathy acted like she was going to help him.

"Don't' even try it whore." Deborah said in a calm voice.

Richard threw the keys, and Deborah caught them.

Cathy raised her fist at me.

"Little girl, I will rip off your head and pee in the hole; don't mess with me."

Deborah and I drove away slowly. We had lunch on the east side and had a nice laugh.

Later in the month, a childhood friend calls.

"When my man was cheating on me, every person in my circle knew but would not tell me because they wanted to stay out of my business. I felt terrible when I found out the hard way."

She continued.

"I saw Ricard in your car last month and he picked up a prostitute on Mack and Bewick. I didn't want you to be the last to know, your man was cheating on you while using your car."

"Thank you, I believe you girl. He's out of my life, I wish I had known this about a month ago, I would have kicked his teeth out." We laughed.

"Darn it, I can't win, this blind-in-one eye, ugly man was the biggest man-whore I've ever met." Karma was my friend. He married Pug nose. He hoed around on her until he couldn't. Then he went completely blind, she was leading him around.

Lesson learned: Watch those so-called female friends because most of the times, his little head will overrule the one on his shoulders.

DRAFT

BITTER SWEET MARRIAGE

I licked my wounds from Richard and chilled out from dating for about 2 years. I stayed busy with Community Theater and an occasional class working towards my MBA.

I met Ken Lamont at Floods in downtown Detroit. He was a cute, paper bag brown brother. Well dressed, tall, and arrogant. This man smelled so fresh and clean. He's an investment banker and deep into rebuilding Detroit.

"So what are you doing trying to rebuild Detroit?"

"I buy old houses, and make them livable and only charge a small price to anyone who purchases it."

"Hum mm, this guy could be on to something." I thought.

"I am also one of the new republicans who will change the party."

I went to one of those boring republican meetings.

We were together five years. He was supportive and came to all of my events. My mother and brother just adored him. Sex was great. I had never known such tenderness and attention to detail during sex. Each interaction, I came two or three times. He blew my mind. We went on vacations together. We spent a week in Hawaii for my birthday. We spent two weeks in Europe just touring around. Our daily schedules were synced, and we were in a routine which made it convenient for both of us.

He was the entire package I prayed for. He gives lots of gifts, and he showers me with compliments. He never comes to my house empty handed. I was truly his Queen.

One night I prayed to God: "Lord I'm getting older, if Ken does want to marry me at the end of five years, please make it plain to me."

Be careful what you pray for; God is listening and sometimes He has a sense of humor. I threw a ladies only birthday party for my Mom.

Ken called to tell her happy birthday.

My cousin Liz was my mother's first cousin. They were raised as sisters. I believe my middle name Elizabeth honors her. She was older, about 6 feet 2 and had the longest fingernails I've ever seen. She dressed moderately and kept to herself. Her hair was wavy like a natural curl. Back in the day, Liz would keep a switchblade between her breasts. Mom said Liz knows how to pull it out, open it and slice a person and put it away in a few seconds and walk away like nothing happened.

"Who is she talking to?" Liz asked.

"My friend, Ken Lamont." I said proudly because he was featured in the papers because he was thinking of running for Mayor of Detroit.

"Oh, I know him; he just married my coworker a few months ago."

My heart dropped into my belly and started beating hard and hurried. My stomach started to quiver and I felt light-headed. No Lord not again. The room was spinning and quiet, all eyes are on me. People started moving in slow motion.

"Ken Lamont, Investment Banker, well-dressed guy?"

"Yep that's him" Liz said.

"What, we've been dating for 5 years."

Liz intuitively knew I was about to reveal more than I should.

"Come by the house tomorrow, we will talk in detail." Then she pulled me close and whispered in my ear, "I will show you pictures."

I could not wait to get off work and rush over to her house. As sure as water was wet, there he was as the groom in the pictures. I left Liz's house and found it difficult to drive because I couldn't see through the tears.

I cried for hours. I felt sick with my broken heart. I threw up a few times. Then mad-mad Maddison" started plotting a creative way to tell him I knew.

I called Ken. "Hi babe, what are you doing?"

"Oh, nothing, just thinking of you."

"Aww, that's sweet. Hey, why don't you come by tonight, I need some special attention."

He got excited. "Oh Maddie, you know I can't resist you, I'll be there at 7:00."

"OK, see you then."

I was wearing a tight-fitting red low cut dress showing lots of cleavage and my small waist. I have on my body shaper, and my butt was popping from all of those squats at the gym.

Ken walked in, sharp as a tack, straight out of a men's fashion magazine. Three piece suit, from Neiman Marcus. His custom-tailored shirt with his initials on the cuff shows off his diamond stud cufflinks that framed the look. The Tie and little hankie matching. His shoes look they were spit shined by the military.

"Hi Cutie, I picked up some of that Gourmet popcorn you love, from Royal Popcorn Company on Gratiot. I could not decide between Hennessy Cognac and Crown Royal Apple, so I got you a large bag of both. I got Banana Pudding popcorn for us later tonight."

"Hey baby, thank you for the popcorn" I said with a sweet smile. "Why don't you sit down right here." I patted the center of the couch and gave him a peck on the lips.

"So how was your day?" I wiggled my shoulders and easily slipped under his arm.

"It was a normal day, lots of work, but I enjoyed it."

"I talked to a friend of mine who went to a wedding."

"Oh yes, who got married?"

"I think her name was Ivy." I said and waited for his reaction. He didn't bat an eye. I went further to bait the hook.

"Do you know a girl named Ivy?" I said as I poured the wine in the glasses.

"Hum mm, let me think, nope I don't think so."

Oh, no he didn't. I thought.

"My friend said it was a picturesque setting on the water at the Yacht Club. It was very well attended and almost like royalty."

I think I'm getting to him. He put down his glass of wine.

"So when was this wedding?"

"I'm not sure, but my friend works at Henry Ford Hospital with Ivy, and they are friends."

"Well, sounds like they had a wonderful wedding."

I am thinking "This bold faced liar didn't even blink, flicker or stutter. Oh, he was good."

"So, who did this Ivy girl marry?" He asks as he sips his wine.

I stand up and face him. "She married you." I said and smiled.

"Madison, what are you saying, this was crazy, I didn't get married." He laughs.

I pulled out a picture, slammed it down on the table like I'm playing dominos.

"Bam; here is a picture of you at the altar with Ivy. Now explain that."

"Oh girl, I can see how you might think I got married. Ivy's husband is my friend and he couldn't make it to the wedding, I stood in for him, it's that simple. Now don't let your imagination run away with you. Young lady, you are acting crazy." He says like I am irritating him.

He stood up, straightens his tie and said. "I made dinner reservations at the Rattlesnake club are you ready to go."

Was he trying to switch this around to make me think I was wrong for asking questions? I got another picture; I had to finish throwing down the domino pictures.

"Do you think I am boo-boo the fool, you married her, and you are still coming to me?"

Slam, slam, two more pictures.

"Get out of my house and never come back."

"Maddie, please believe me it's not me, I would never hurt you. I love you. I want to marry you."

I looked him square in the eyes without a smile or showing any emotion, and I said; "If you don't leave now I will reach behind the couch, get my gun and blow off that thing you call a penis."

I took a breath and calmly said. "Your choice, stay or go."

He picked up his keys and left. I cried every day for about a week. I was deceived for five years. I believed we had something real.

When I could not cry anymore, I played a song the song "I cried my last tear yesterday". I must have played it a zillion times on a loop until I didn't feel the pain.

I have to sever all ties with him. Ken talked me into buying a Certificate of Deposit (CD) it was set to mature, giving me 12% return on my investment. I called the phone number to cancel it.

I looked at the signature of the witness. The name was Ivy Lamont. This will never do. Mad-mad Madison was coming out to play.

I called his main office number.

"Hello, may I speak to the person in charge of the short term CD's".

"Yes, Miss, you are speaking with Mr. Brown, how may I help you?" The man on the other end said with a soft businesslike voice.

"Mr. Brown, I would like to cash out my CD."

"Well, Miss you will not get the entire 12% if you pull out now, it has not matured."

"I am aware of that, but I would whether take a loss than to have to deal with Mr. Lamont again, I am terrified of him."

"What do you mean?" I could tell I had his undivided attention.

"What I mean was he came to my house unannounced saying I forgot to sign some papers. Then he said he was attracted to me and was going to have sex with me and I would enjoy it. Sir, he made me uncomfortable. I had to threaten him to get him out of my house. I am petrified of him. He also mentioned he uses drugs and had some he would give me to enhance the sex. I strongly suggest you give him a drug test before he sees any more clients."

I sniffed a few times as if I was crying. I made my voice drop like I was hurt and just could not carry on. He was buying my Oscar-winning performance hook, line and sinker.

"Ok, ok, calm down Miss. This is what I will do for you; I will give you the amount you put into the CD. You will not have to pay the penalties for cashing out early.

In addition, you can believe Mr. Lamont will be dealt with of regarding his actions. Do you wish to bring formal charges?"

"Oh no. I don't ever want to see him again, please don't mention my name and don't tell him I told you. He might come back. I am terrified of him. Thank you."

As I hang up I thought, He will get what he deserves. He was such a pig.

Lesson learned: In an established relationship don't get in a rut. I should be able to interrupt his schedule and be his priority at any moment of any day.

THE CHURCH CHOIR

After Ken, I was off the market for about a year. I needed to get my head straight and get this anger out of my system. I started taking night classes at Wayne State University towards my MBA to keep my mind occupied.

I became more active in my church. It was time to stop being a bench member and do something. I stepped in choir rehearsal like a nervous cat. The choir director was a small, pompous older lady who smells like the cream you put on sore muscles. She had blue tinted hair. She was dressed in a sweat suit.

"Hello, what can I do for you today?" She greeted me.

"I want to join the choir, I sing Soprano."

"I will let you know what you sing after you audition."

I'm thinking "Dang, she was cold-blooded. I didn't know you had to audition for a come as you are church choir. This chick was about to piss me off up-in-here with her attitude of I am better than you.

"OK mam" I said and smiled.

"Honey, you just sit down right here and listen. I will get to your audition in a minute." She said without looking at me and pointed to the front pew facing the choir stand.

No, this heifer didn't have me sing in front of the whole choir. The organist played a note; I hit it. He kept escalating, and surprisingly I hit the notes. He went up two octaves. The last one was extremely high. I took a deep breath and belted it out. When I finished, every choir member was clapping with approval.

"You are a soprano, go sit over there." Little Miss heifer said in a snotty voice.

Choir rehearsal was therapeutic in keeping me calm and kept mad-mad Madison under lock and key.

I prayed every night for God to keep me calm, and more important, keep stupid people out of my way while I was trying to get right.

One Tuesday while in choir rehearsal I noticed the same people leading the songs. I didn't say anything because I know I can't lead a song. Jean who always sits next to me can really blow.

"Jean, why don't you lead any songs?" I ask when Little Miss Heifer was giving the altos their notes.

"Girl, they have their favorites, if you are not in the click, you don't get to lead."

I was shocked. "Are you kidding me, favoritism happens in here?"

"Honey, open your eyes. That is why only a select few people lead songs and they are the relatives or friends of the music staff. The organist is the director's son. The piano player is married to the organist daughter and the drummer is the director's grandson."

This put a rotten taste in my mouth. I talked to Little Miss Heifer after rehearsal.

"Ms. Director, why is it only a few people lead all of the songs?"

"Honey, do you want to lead a song?"

"Maybe, what do I need to do?"

"You have to have the ability to hold your own, and from what I hear from you, you can't do that."

I was thinking; "Oh, snap, no she didn't just go there. Come on Jesus; keep my tongue and my hands still."

"Thank you Ms. Director, but there are others in the choir who can hold their own and should be given the opportunity to lead a song."

"Are you serious, I didn't know that, the next time we have a new song, I will ask someone to volunteer for the lead."

"What an excellent idea, thank you for listening to me." I said, thankful that I have made a difference and others will have an opportunity to lead songs.

Needless to say, it never happened. Every time a song was taught, the leader was singing the lead part while the choir was learning their part. We would rehearse a song for an hour. I would go home and practice every day to make sure I knew my part. On Sunday we would sing a completely different song.

The choir members started treating me like I had Leprosy. I was alienated and no one talked to me. All I did was speak up. I never looked at the choir the same.

I lost my zest; I lost my faith in the choir. I lost my avenue to calm. I lost my willingness to give up a Tuesday night for this Bull.

"Bench Member Ministry, here I come again." Church hurt is real.

Lesson learned: Even churches have clicks. The church is like a hospital for all people. There is no perfect church. My calm and acceptance will have to come from God not the people in the church.

FAMILY CHALLENGES

Mom called "What are you doing? Why don't you come by the house for dinner?"

"Ok sure"

This was odd, why was she inviting me over, and it's not Sunday.

My brother was there too.

"Forget the food, what's going on?"

"Oh, Madison, you are always direct and to the point, let's socialize for a little while." Mom said.

"OK, we are having nice weather, and the Pistons won a couple of games. Now, what's going on?"

My mom moved closer to my dad, they held hands and she said.

"Your father has lung cancer and they don't expect him to live more than five months."

"Oh no, no. What can we do, this is not true, how did this happen? We can use alternative methods, we can fight this." I said in disbelief.

"Calm yourself down little girl, there is more." Mom said,

"More, what else can there be?"

"Baby, they discovered a lump in my breast, and I will have to have the breast removed."

"My God, this is too much. How long have you guys known about your medical conditions? Did you get second and third opinions?"

I felt faint; I looked at Jacob to get some kind of support. This fool was texting on his cell phone.

"Boy." I yelled.

"Did you hear what mom said?"

"No, not really, I figured you were listening and would tell me if it was important."

I gave him a look like "If eyes could burn, you would be crisp."

"Jacob, they both have cancer and Dad might die in 5 months."

Jacob stands up and was too weak, and falls back in the chair sobbing.

"I can't breathe, I can't breathe, and somebody get me some water."

"Jacob, man up and gather yourself. We have to be there for them."

"Who do you think you talking to; I am not your child."

"Well, my brother, you are acting like one."

"Stop it. Can we have a little peace for once?" Mom scolds us.

The next five months were exhausting. Dad was in the hospital a lot. After work, I went by the hospital for a couple of hours. After the hospital, I went to school.

"Hi Dad, how are you doing?"

"Oh baby girl, I have seen better days. I just want you to know, I appreciate you coming by every day to check on me."

"Dad, it's a rare privilege to do this small thing for you considering all the stuff you've done for me my entire life. I am a daddy's girl and there is a special bond between us, I love you. I will always be here for you."

"I know you are my rock Madison. Your brother has not called or been to the hospital at all, and your mother is dealing with her health issues, she comes when she can."

The nurse name Pat came in. I appreciate the way he takes care of my dad. He was loving, extremely efficient, personable and the best nurse around. Not to mention a great sense of humor and a lot of fun. He was tall, with blond hair blue eyes. One day we had a conversation about gay marriage.

"Yep, you guys should get married. You can get divorced and be miserable like the rest of us." I told him.

He got a belly laugh out of that.

"Honey Chile, visiting hours are over, you don't have to go home, but you have to leave here."

"Well, all righty then. Pat, I appreciate the way you are taking care of my dad. I can rest comfortably because I know you are here."

"Thank you, you know I've got your back. Now get out of here."

I kiss Dad on the forehead. "Goodnight Dad."

"Good night baby, make sure you check on your mom tomorrow." Dad says gasping for breath.

"OK, I will, don't worry about anything, rest well."

While driving home, I call Jacob on the cell phone.

"What is wrong with you? You have not gone to see Dad?"

"All girl calm down, you know I don't like hospitals."

"Jacob, it is not pleasant for me either. His illness is not about what you like and don't like. Get a grip; it's not always about you. He needs to feel the love from us because his time is short. Now promise me, you will go tomorrow."

"Yah, whatever, I guess I can swing by for a minute."

That night, mom called from his hospital room, Dad passed away. I rushed to the hospital, Dad was peaceful and still. He was not cold yet. Mom was quiet and looking at me while I was looking at Dad.

Then it hit me; my daddy was gone. I got weak and had to sit down. I sobbed, and the nurses brought tissues. I'm thinking. "I knew he was going to die, but I can't stop crying."

Then someone said "We are often prepared, but never ready to let a loved one go." My chest was pounding; my head was beating rhythmically with my chest. All of the machines are gone. People were moving and talking in slow motion. All I heard were quiet muffled sounds.

"What are we supposed to do now?" I asked.

I've never had to deal with this. I looked at mom, she was as still as death itself. I'm hoping this stress does not kick up her breast cancer issues. Jacob did not come to the hospital that night. He was a first class butt-hole.

"I understand I have 24 hours to make arrangements, and I will comply." Mom told the nurses. Then we left.

I spent the night with mom. She went right to bed without any conversation. The next morning, while she was cooking breakfast, I studied her. Obviously she had been up for a while. She was fully dressed, hair comb and as beautiful as ever. She had an eerie calmness; I think she was in shock.

They were married for 30 years; Dad treated her like a queen. If we crossed her, we had to prepare for his wrath. If Dad thought mom wanted something, he would save his money until he could buy it for her. When the family sat down for dinner and wanted seconds or something from the kitchen he would say "Get it yourself; my wife is enjoying her dinner too." Without fail, after each meal, he would kiss her and tell her "That was delicious, you put your foot in it mint." Mint was his pet name for her like the sweet mint julep drink. Then he would bring her a glass of Ice water.

"Mom, don't worry, I can help you with the planning."

"Don't you worry little missy, we planned this together." She says with a slight smile.

"As Rickey would say; Splain Lucy, Splain." I question her.
"Well, miss know-it-all. You know we are praying people, and God wants all things done decently and in order. We knew there was an appointed time and this day would come.

Years ago, we took out a pre-needs policy on both of us with Butler Funeral home. The Casket, flowers and all things necessary are picked out and paid for. The church secretary has the program the funeral will be in one week." She says with confidence.

"I didn't know you guys were this organized. What can I do to help you?"

"Baby, you can start calling the relatives and friends with the details."

"No problem, I am on it." I was glad to do something to keep busy and not think about my dad.

I found their torn and taped up address book and started the process. I posted it on Facebook. The phone started ringing.

"No, mom, I will answer the calls, you get some rest and if you think of something I need to do, just let me know."

"Girl, you aren't my momma I am yours. During this time, I don't want to deny those who care about me the opportunity to give an encouraging word. Trust me, I need this. If I just sit around and think about my husband, I will go crazy. I need the support of those who love me."

"Ok, you know you. If it gets overbearing, just let me know."

About 5:00 pm Jacob drove up, music blasting Motown oldies. He walked in dressed in a black and white sweat suit; Knowing, he has never seen the inside of a gym.

"Where have you been? You know mom needs our support now."

"Get off my back." he said, then turned and walked away.

"Oh, I know what's going on in your head, it is called guilt. You are feeling guilty because you didn't visit Dad in the hospital or do anything to comfort him."

He looked at me emotionless. I got a chill. He starts walking fast towards me. I'm thinking; "If he wants to fight, I will sweep the floor with his trifling butt."

Just before he reaches me, he stretches out his arms for a hug and starts to sob uncontrollably. He falls on my shoulders, and I struggle to hold him up. Tears and snot are flying everywhere.

"Madison, I am sorry for the way I treated Dad. I lied to him. I purposely disobeyed him. I know he was just trying to teach me to be a man. I am sorry."

"What are you talking about?"

"I know he didn't tell you and mom this story; When was sick and weak, I challenged him. We had a fist fight."

I pushed him away.

"You did what? You worthless, selfish piece of dirt."

"No, Maddie let me finish."as What had happened was…., I put up my fists. I took my stand and swung hard at him and missed. He hit me and I hit the floor.

My jaw felt like a train hit me. I thought he knocked out all of my teeth. I crawled out of the house and got in my car and drove away. I didn't hurt him physically, but I could see the hurt in his eyes when he hit me. That was why I didn't go to the hospital; I was too ashamed and could not face him."

"Your pitiful butt was wrong on all levels. I heard when boys start to smell themselves they will challenge their fathers. I guess you did too. What I don't like is you waited until he was sick. Hell is not hot enough for you Jacob.

Go wash your face and blow your nose before you see mom."

The three of us sat at the table. Jacob looked kind of sheepish and asked about the program for the funeral.

"Mom had it done months ago and the church secretary has it, it's a wrap."

"We have to add something."

"What are you talking about fool?"

"Please don't be mad."

"You better start talking; I am losing my patience with you."

"You know Emily and I have been dating for about 5 years now…."

"Oh naw, to the naw no, she will not be in the obituary as a family member." I said waving my index finger and doing the snakehead.

"Maddie just shut up and let me finish". Jacob said.

"Ok, go ahead."

"Here it is. I forgot to tell you, she got pregnant, and we have triplets."

Mom and I said in unison "What! Triplets?"

"Details, Jacob, Details. You know you didn't forget to tell us. When were they born? When were you going to tell us? What are their names, we want to see them. This is a new low even for you. Dad was a grandfather, and you denied him that privilege. I should put my foot so far up in your butt; it will take you until next week to get it out." I said.

In a calm voice, mom said. "Call Emily and ask her to bring them over. I could use some innocent cheering up. I am upset with of you for keeping this from me. Yes, I am disappointed you didn't wait until you were married. You had no right to keep my grandchildren a secret. What's done is done, call Emily son."

Emily has butt for days. I didn't know there were clothes to fit her Texas-sized butt. She has breast the size of raisins, a gigantic belly and skinny legs. She is half Hispanic and half African American with a golden brown complexion. Such a cute face; long eyelashes and she keeps her hair cut short.

Back in the day, she had coke pop-bottom glasses because her vision is horrible. Now, she wears green contacts hoping somebody believes her eyes are green.

She had no conversation except complaining all of the time. Lord, don't mention eating healthy or going to the gym; she closes up like a jail cell on lockdown.

Emily pulled up, and Jacob went to meet her. I peeked out the window. They have two girls and a boy who looks to be about a year old. It surprised me that Jacob was tender and caring towards her and the kids. "That trifling fool, how could he not tell us?"

"Hi girl, great to see you, it's been a while." I said to Emily.

"Yes, it has."

"So why didn't you tell us about these kids?" I began the interrogation.

"Stop Madison, there will be time for those questions, let's just enjoy them for now." Mom says.

"OK."

"Jacob, will you introduce me to my grandchildren."

"This is Kimberly, this is Kayla, and this is Cameron."

"How did you come up with those names" I asked

"We looked on the Internet"

"Wait, the names are not passed down through the family, you just went on the Internet, and did a point and click."

"Madison, its fine." Mom says.

I must admit, the three musketeers are cute.

Mom called the church secretary and asked her to revise the obituary to include her grandchildren.

PERFECT HOSTESS

Dad's funeral was packed. People I had not seen in years. I know they came to see who attended, and see how my dad looked. Some just came for the free food at the repass.

Lord, please get these people out of my mother's house. They are eating all the food, cracking jokes and asking me to wait on them. One preacher indicated he does not drink water out of a paper cup and demanded a glass. I'm thinking "this is how you comfort me in the loss of my dad, please just go, we will be fine."

I can't believe who showed up it was Ken Lamont with his wife Ivy.

"Hello, Ken."

"Hi Madison, this is my wife Ivy. I've always respected your dad and still care about your mother."

"Thank you for coming, mom is over there." I said and kept walking. I sure wanted to ask him if he lost his job because of my phone call.

Richard and Cathy were behind them.

"Hi Richard, it's Madison, I heard you were completely blind now." I said in a compassionate voice.

"Yes, but Cathy has been taking care of me."

"Isn't that sweet? My mother is sitting over there. Cathy, will you take him to her please?"

These two need to stop. Here comes bad hair Becky along with Myrtle. I could just slap Myrtle for being friends with the chick who was openly having an affair with her husband, the dog Andrew. I greeted them with open arms. "Hi ladies, it means a lot that you came to support us. Thank you for coming."

Here come the representatives from the choir; Jean and Little Miss Heifer, the choir director.

"Oh, Madison, we are sorry for your loss." Little Miss Heifer said in a failed attempt at being compassionate.

"Thank you, I appreciate you coming by."

They shook hands with each person and they were out in less than 5 minutes."

My goodness, I was extremely tired and running on fumes.

Who was this strange man rushing towards me with his hand extended?

"Sorry for your loss." He says with a firm handshake.

"Thank you for your kindness."

"You don't remember me do you?"

"No, I don't."

"Well, back in the day I was not nice to you." He says as he tilted his head down and flashed a half smile.

"Oh snap, are you Donald Blink, the school bully?"

"In the flesh."

"How did you know about my father?"

"Madison, I'm still in the neighborhood and I've kept up with your family from a distance. I would like you to meet my wife, Carol."

"I am glad you both came. It is nice to see Donald finally grew up."

We all laugh.

"Please excuse me. I have to check on my mother. Go fix yourself a plate."

As I passed the buffet table, Noah was there with a plate of food piled up like a pyramid. I waved and smiled, but did not give him the opportunity to say anything. As far as I'm concerned, he could put his "I'm sorry for your loss" in a card.

I was exhausted. After I checked on mom, I went to the back room to rest and flop down in dad's recliner. I threw my head back and closed my eyes. After a minute or two, I open my eyes to see this fine man who has a face like a male angel tucked in the corner. He was flawless.

His hair looked like the barber put every hair in place individually. His full thick beard was shaped, trimmed and groomed to perfection. His nails are manicured and neat.

He had his jacket across his knee. Lord have mercy! The tight-fitting shirt showed the biceps and every curved muscle in his arms. He obviously works out.

What was happening to me, my heart started pounding, my throat got dry and my hands started sweating. I wanted to introduce myself, but I could not move. I couldn't stop staring at this man. He got up and was walking in my direction. He extended his hand.

"Hello Madison"

I melted at the sound of his booming bass voice.

"Do I know you? How do you know my name?"

"My name is Drake. You don't know me, but I live next door to Emily and I helped her and Jacob bring in the water and food. I hope you don't mind, I fixed myself a plate."

"No not at all, have as much as you like." I said, trying to maintain my composure.

"Thank you. If it's ok, may I will take this seat next to you?"

"Oh, please do."

"It looks like your father was well loved."

"Yes, he was. He was a Trustee at the church and a foreman at the Auto Plant. I am or should I say was a daddy's girl. It hurts to know I won't see him again. I don't think it's hit me yet. My Pastor told me there are the five stages of grief that I have to go through in order to heal."

"Oh, that's interesting, please go on." He said, while looking at me straight in the eye.

Then it happened, enormous butt Emily walked past with her gigantic butt sister. They came into my space like Two Tons of Jell-O sloshing around. There were butts and thighs jiggling north and south, then east and west. Her sister does not have a man but can tell you all you should and shouldn't do with yours.

The three musketeers were screaming and running after them. There goes my peaceful retreat.

Drake kept his focus on me like we were the only ones in the room.

"What?? A black man who does not watch for the dunk-a-dunk, double bounce of a big butt? Aww, don't tell me he's gay." I thought.

Just then, Drake took my hand, looked into my eyes and said, "We don't have to talk about it now, please tell me more about you." I darn near fell out of the recliner. His touch gave me chills and aroused me at the same time.

We talked for hours unaware of who coming or going into the back room. He seemed interested in my job at Ford Motor Company as an IT specialist. He was an Electrical Engineer with Chrysler.

"It's getting late, and I must leave in order to get my rest for work tomorrow. I hope I'm not being too forward if I ask for your phone number." He said.

"Why don't I take your number and I will give you mine when I verify you are not a serial killer." We laughed, and then he wrote his number on a napkin.

I spent the night with mom. She was drained and went to bed while the guests were still there.

"It's OK, mom, these people know you are tired and have been through a lot. Your chemo treatments will begin soon. You need your rest."

Ten minutes after she went to bed, I politely asked everybody to leave. I could not sleep, I thought about Drake all night. I got on my knees and prayed.

"Lord, you know we just buried my dad and I feel empty. There was a hole in my chest I can't touch. I adored and respected him. Lord, I need a favor. I would like to call you daddy. I need that extra love a daddy gives his child. A daddy takes care and protects, as you have done for me all of my life. I am your child. I feel much closer to you when I call you daddy."

"Daddy, I am worried about my mother, please touch her body and make her whole, touch her heart and help her heal from the loss of my dad."

"Now Lord, you know the mess I've been going through with relationships. I just want to be by myself before I seriously hurt someone. But, Lord, I think I like this guy, Drake. Daddy, please don't let me fall in love with another cheater, looser, or a no good jerk. You made me and you know what I am capable of doing.

I've been going to Sunday School, attending both church services, and the Wednesday bible class. I have been paying attention to what the pastor has been saying. I've been reading my bible every day, watching religious programs on TV and trying to do the right thing. I even read a relationship book, twice.

I listened to the pastor when he taught from James 3:16-18 and Amos 3:3 about identifying a toxic relationship. Lord, I paid attention and have applied what I learned. He said in order to build a healthy relationship; I have to cut off the old ones who push my buttons.

Daddy, I have been faithful to the bench member ministry. I also tried to memorize the identity of love in First Corinthians chapter 13.

Reading your word gives me the calm feeling I've been missing. Daddy, please direct me, I want to stop making these mistakes with men. This I ask in your Son Jesus name, Amen."

After my prayer, I slept like a baby.

STARTING TO TRUST

I waited a couple of days before I called Drake.

"Hello, this is Madison."

"Hi, there I knew it was you."

Just hearing his voice made me like weak in the knees and an unusual sensation over my entire body.

"I really enjoyed our conversation the other day."

"Yeah, me too. Judging from your body language and choice of words, I can tell you've been hurt by these no good brothers."

"Hum mm". I say, becoming skeptical of his observation.

"You are the kind of woman I could really fall for. You are intelligent, no children, drop dead gorgeous, and you have your head on straight. I would really like to spend more quality time with you. I would be pleased if you would be my friend for now."

"That works for me."

"So, my new friend the annual Jazz festival is in downtown Detroit this weekend, are you available?"

"Let me check my schedule, yes, I can make it on Sunday afternoon, after church."

"Alright, may I pick you up at your mother's around 3:00? We can grab a bite to eat, and then go to the festival".

"Ok, sounds like a plan, I will see you Sunday."

It was great. We laughed, talked and acted silly. He shared about his family and how he was raised. He wanted me to know everything about him.

He said "This will make it easy for you to trust me because you will know me completely."

Everything was going well. After about 4 months, I was beginning to let down my walls and trust him a little bit. I even stopped wearing the body shaper on our dates.

THE BIG C

After doing research on mom's breast cancer, I found out the US Government has known about a cure for all cancers since 1938 but did not want the doctors to use it because it's all natural and the pharmaceutical companies would not survive. I actually saw a photo of a bottle of the chemo. It clearly states its cacogenic; meaning it causes cancer. My friend Arnold told me how he cured himself of cancer.

The Internet revealed a nurse named Rene Caisse who developed a cure, and it's called Essiac (her name spelled backwards) The government acknowledged her cure worked between the years of 1920 and 1970, but they shut her down because of the pharmaceutical companies. Essiac was still sold over the Internet. Also, many people are being cured with cannabis oil.

I found a YouTube on Dr. Sabi. The government took him to the Supreme Court because he said he cured Cancer, Aids and a lot of *diseases*. He won his case because he proved he cured a lot of people based on the reports from their doctors. He was found dead in police custody in 2016. I approached Mom with alternative solutions to chemo and radiation.

"Mom, I want you to take a look at these YouTube videos and tell me what you think."

"Girl ain't nobody got time for that. What was this about?"

"It's about finding alternative methods to clean all the cells in your body and get rid of the cancer."

"Sho'noff. It can be done outside of the hospital?"

"Yes, Cancer is a fungus and not a virus. We have to change your diet to anti-fungal foods. You have to eliminate sugar because cancer feeds off of sugar. We are going to get rid of the dairy because it causes mucus which is a breeding ground for cancer. You will have to work out too. Mom, I know you don't like pills, but you will have to take two Vitamin C pills every four hours.

"What? Why do I have to do that?"

"Vitamin C is one of the best things to keep cancer at bay. Don't worry; we can put them in the morning smoothie."

"OK, I guess I can set the timer on my phone to take the Vitamin C."

"Wonderful Mom! Now you are thinking. The goal is to get the right Ph Balance in your body.

Guess what, there is a doctor in Canada who injects baking soda in the tumor in the breast and the tumor shrinks or disappears. What do you think about trying an alternative method to chemo?"

"Honey yes, we can give it a try. We can empty the pantry of all of the unwanted food and then we can go shopping. Do I have to exercise every day?"

"Yes, you do."

"I am not doing a spin class or all of that jumping up and down stuff in Zumba."

"You don't have to. We will start with a brisk walk every morning to get your heart pumping."

"Agreed, I can do that." She said with a smile.

"Mom, one last thing. I saw online where a lot of people are being cured by taking cannabis oil."

"What is that?"

"Well, it's from the marijuana plant."

"Now hold it right there, I'm not going to be a dope addict. I am not going to try that stuff."

"Alright, we will stick with the other solutions."

Mom told her Integrative Oncologist what she planned to do. They confirmed they heard about the alternatives but under law could not recommend them. They still wanted to monitor her monthly.

Each morning before work when something was not falling from the sky in Detroit, I picked her up. We walked the Dequindre Cut for about a mile. When it was raining, we walked around the mall.

This was our bonding time, and I enjoyed my special time with her. We talked about Dad and how much she missed him. She helped me to understand Jacob and the three musketeers.

I could see her getting stronger and actually enjoying walking. She had been shopping and bought some jazzy workout clothes. One morning she shocked me.

"Baby, tell me again about the doctor in Canada and the banking soda stuff. I saw something online and it sounds interesting."

I repeated the story.

"Madison, let's go to Canada, it's only across the bridge."

"Mom are you serious? Yes, let's do this. Get your records from your Oncologist and I will contact the doctor in Canada."

We had an appointment in a week. As we walked into the magnificently designed office, we were greeted with smiles by an incredibly polite staff. These young, slender 20 something car-pool moms were quite accommodating. There was Starbucks coffee and tea available. Fresh fruit was on the coffee table.

The office was painted in pastels and gravitation from one color to another without a sharp interruption of color. I couldn't find the fuser that emitted a sweet smell of Jasmine. It felt more like a spa than a doctor's office. The hardwood floors were spotless; you could eat off of them. We sat in leather massaging recliners. I fell asleep because I felt my head do the "bobble head" jerk.

In an effort to save time, we filled out the paperwork online and emailed it. They verified her identification and other requested information.

Dr. Simmons came to the waiting room and personally escorted us into his office. He was a tall white guy in his 40's. You can tell he works out. I can see his large biceps and triceps through his white coat. He had exceptionally clear piercing light blue eyes.

On his desk, he had pictures of his wife who has an asymmetrical short dark hair cut. He has a boy and a girl who are hugging a Labrador retriever. My guess was they have a white picket fence too.

"I've read your paperwork and reviewed your chart. Your X-rays and scans clearly show you have a Tubular Carcinoma of the Breast. The good news is it has not reached the lymph nodes yet." He said.

"Yes, we have been told that. Now can you tell us something we don't know?" I said in a matter of fact tone.

"Madison stop that. Please go on Doctor."

"We can do the baking soda injection. It will definitely slow the growth of the tumor because we will change the environment where it thrives."

A catheter is used to administer sodium bicarbonate through the arteries directly into the tumor; in a suggested ratio of 500 ml x 5% sodium bicarbonate for a period of 6 days on, 6 days off for a total of 4 cycles to completion. This method has a 99% success rate for healing Breast Cancer."

The combination of the anti-fungal foods, exercise, the bicarbonate injections, and Vitamin C, mom was cancer free according to Dr. Simmons and her Oncologist.

She testified in church, and we had a shouting good time. She realized taking care of her body was her present and future situation. Now she is taking Ballroom dancing classes with Mr. Smooth. She's got her Ballroom groove back on.

RELOCATING

For two years, I was wined and dined by Drake. He bought gifts at least once a month. We even went on the Mr. Smooth Ball Room Dancers Cruise. Never once did he try to force himself on me sexually. He knew what I had gone through with past relationships and I was celibate and waiting until I got married. I was content he understood.

While at a picnic at Bell Island, Drake dropped a bomb.

"I've been promoted, and I have to move to California."

I was numb. I heard the "dunn dunn" sound from Law and Order.

"What? When?" I asked.

He put my face in his hands and held me close and said.

"Maddie, I have never said this to you before, but you know I love you. And I am pretty sure you love me."

I just looked into his stunning eyes and softened.

"Baby, why don't we get married and you come to California with me." Then he kissed me tenderly.

"Is that a proposal? Where is the ring? What about getting on one knee? Drake are you really serious?"

"Honey, if you want all that, I will make it happen, but right now I just want to know, what do you think about marrying me?"

"You know I love you, but this is a lot to process. I can't leave my mother. I don't want to lose you. I can transfer my job there. I would like to go to California to be with you. Babe, I've wanted to marry you from the first moment I saw you. My thoughts are racing. Please just hold me for a few minutes, I need to process this."

We embraced for about 10 minutes in silence.

"Please take me home." I whispered in his ear.

I called my mother.

"Mom, I don't want to leave you. I know Jacob will not be as attentive as I am. Emily and the triplets are taking all of his time."

"You have to live your life. I cannot tell you to go, and I cannot tell you to stay. But I will tell you that I am happy and healthy.

Don't worry about me, I will be fine. Pray about it and listen for God's voice to instruct you. From what he's shown me, Drake is a fine young man. Baby, recognize the feeling deep down in your belly. It is the best indicator when something is not as it appears."

"Yes Mam"

I told Drake Yes. He was beyond excited as he got on one knee and presented my ring; a blinding five-carat halo diamond surrounded with Baguettes'.

Drake's job demanded him to move to California six months before the wedding. I continued to plan the wedding and make sure all of my paperwork was in place for my Job transfer.

We talked at length two or three times a day. I knew his every move and he knew mine. He found a house in Torrance on Park Street. He emailed the purchase details pictures. It was an enchanting two-story green colonial with a white picket fence not far from Pacific Coast Highway. The best part of the house was the Laundry room was on the 2nd floor between the bedrooms.

We had a large wedding. My feet never touched the ground. The wedding night was magical. After love making, he cried and told me how much he loved me and he was thankful I waited for him.

It took four months after the wedding for the transfer and move to Torrance California. Although it was expensive, during those four months, Drake would fly home other every month.

Each time, it was like we were newlyweds all over again. He would explode in my body which made me feel the most amazing total body experience. I love me some him.

Finally, it was time for me to move. My house is sold, and the job transfer came through. I will be a Purchasing Agent at a Ford Parts Distribution Center. My MBA credits transferred from Wayne State to Pepperdine University.

Drake flew in and, the two of us pack up my whole house in one week. With all of the packing and planning, I noticed Drake was not as affectionate and attentive as normal. We only made love once and it didn't seem like love, just "wham bam, thank you mam."

The movers are taking the home furnishings and we are driving my Lincoln.

It was heart-wrenching saying by to mom. Jacob called and said he does not like goodbyes and to call him when I get to California.

It was about a 2,000 mile drive. Drake drove, stopping every 5 hours to stretch and for rest in a hotel. We had casual conversations.

"So, honey, how is the job situation coming along?"

"What do you mean job situation?"

"I mean the job. What's going on? What do you like about it, and what don't you like? Tell me about the friends you've made? When are you going to take me where you work, I want to see you in your zone?"

"Now hold your horses, you are always rapid fire on the questions. The job is going fine. That's all you need to know."

"What's wrong with you? No need to get short with me."

"Sorry babe, I'm just tired from all of the driving, I apologize." He reaches and squeezes my hand.

"Apology accepted. Baby, maybe we should pull into a hotel, you need to get some rest."

"There you go again, always trying to tell me what to do. I will pull over when I am ready to pull over."

"Fine, I am going to take a nap, you just be extra careful while driving."

"Shut up and go to sleep woman."

"Drake, I don't like your tone, you can't talk to me any kind of way."

"I can talk to you any way I choose, you are my wife now."
My head was spinning. I have never seen this side of him. Was this exhaustion or the beginning of a life of disrespect and walking on eggshells? We spent the next 3 days driving and stopping with little conversation.

I read a book with my headphones on. He had the music blasting and only turned it down when one of his friends called. No consideration for me. Finally, we arrive home.

"Oh honey, it is nicer than the pictures you sent." I said with a lot of excitement.

He replied, "I know I just love it. Come on; let me give you the grand tour then you can start spending my money to decorate the way you want."

To my surprise, it was decorated with spectacular detail. It was my color scheme, all the way down to the towels in the guest restroom on the ground floor. The living room and dining room looked like a model to a new development.

"Drake, this is nice. Did the sellers leave this stuff, or did you buy it?

"No babe, I got it. I know what you like and just wanted it to be nice for you."

"Good job sweetheart."

"Well, you won't think that when you get upstairs to the bedrooms."

He was right. There was just a bed and his clothes. The master bath was a mess.

"No worries, I will have fun decorating this place."

We unloaded the car and took a nap.

Since I am directional challenged, even with the GPS, Drake insisted we make two test runs to my job before I started the next week. There are more freeways to get to work than there were driving from Detroit to California.

DRAFT

WORK FLOW

My first day at work was a trip.

I wore my pastel lime green suit with a white silk blouse, nylons and natural color hills. I looked professional and ready to take on the world. Since I had not found a beautician, I did my own natural hair from a YouTube video.

I arrived 15 minutes early and walked in with the confidence my dad taught me. Head up and with a purpose like I own the Mother.

With a smile, I said "Hello, I am Madison, I'm looking for HR." to the first person I met. She was a kind-faced tall older white lady who looked like she stepped out of the 50's. "Yes, we have been expecting you, follow me."

She led me through a long hallway to her office and processed all of the paperwork. Then led me back down that hallway and introduced me to the office manager.

"Jamal, this is Madison, she is our new employee."

He was an attractive older black man about 5 feet 9 inches. Jamal was well dressed in a fine suit. He wore spit-shined Gators.

I noticed the pictures of his wife and his four children. His wedding ring was wide. My guess is his wife wanted to make sure women knew he was married.

"Hi Madison, it is good to have you here. We are expecting great things from you."

"Thank you, Jamal, I am excited about this new chapter in my life."

"Jamal, I will introduce her to the others."

"Please do, thank you." Jamal said as he extended his left arm in the direction of the open space office area like he was an usher in church.

The bullpen was a large office with 3 women who were not fashion savvy. All of them were dressed in a blouse and a skirt, or a blouse and loose-fitting pants. No one had on hills. They were not office casual; they were just plain.

"Excuse me." She announced.

"This is Madison, she transferred from Detroit and she will be working at this desk. Madison, this is Linda, and she will be your supervisor."

"Hello, I am excited to be here and working with you." I said.

Each lady took a turn saying hi. We had some small talk, then Linda led me to my desk and explained my responsibilities.

I wanted to get a cold pop, but when I checked my wallet, I didn't even have a dollar. I could have sworn I put fifty dollars in my purse.

I cherish the dinner table discussions because it was where Drake and I caught up and shared our day.

"Babe, I could have sworn I had some cash in my purse, but when I checked, I didn't even have a dollar."

"I needed some small bills, so I took a little from your wallet."

"Why did you do that and not leave me anything? Please do not go in my purse again."

"Do you have something in there you don't want me to see?"

"No, it's about my privacy."

"OK, I didn't know it was that serious. I will ask the next time."

"Thank you. Now let me tell you about work. The office manager was a black guy who I think is really cool."

"Oh yeah, he knows you're married, right." He said without looking up from his dinner.

"Why do you say that? Of course, he does. What a strange thing to say."

"No, it's not, I know what goes on in the office when fresh meat comes in, let me know if I need to come up there."

"Honey, there is no need for all of that, it is a work environment, pure and simple.

Now let me tell you about my lady supervisor. Her name is Linda she is an older lady who does not realize she has aged. She is about 70 and wears tight miniskirts and see-through blouses. I noticed at the initial introduction; she looked me up and down before she spoke.

Since I don't see any women in suits, they don't wear them and I was way overdressed. Tomorrow, I will leave my suit jacket at home."

"Very wise baby, trying to blend."

"Yep, I will be blending like a super duper Food Processer."

We laugh.

I continued. "I have a budget of $1Million each year. I am responsible for every purchase inside and outside of the building except car parts."

We finished dinner and went to bed.

The next day I arrive at work about 30 minutes early I was first to arrive. I was still learning the traffic patterns. About fifteen minutes later, Linda walks in with a "confident strut" wearing a fitted suit with 5 inch Stelios matching her suit. She puts her purse and lunch on her desk and walks over to my desk.

"Good morning Madison."

"Good Morning Linda, how are you this morning?"

"I'm fine, can't you tell. As you can see, you are not the only one who can dress fashionably. I am the supervisor, and I will be wearing the suits around here."

"Are you serious? Is there a dress code I didn't see in my paperwork?"

"No there is not. Jamal and I felt it was necessary for me to establish myself as the supervisor and I am asking you not to wear a suit jacket."

When Jamal came in, I went into his office.

"Is it a requirement that I do not wear a suit jacket? I have never had a position within the company that dictated this action."

"No it's not a requirement, it is just a request."

"OK, I don't want to start off on the wrong foot, I will comply."

Needless to say, going to Jamal did not sit well with Linda.

I could not wait to share this with Drake at dinner.

"Baby, you won't guess what happened at work today."

"What's going on honey?"

"Linda said she's the only one who will be wearing suits in the office."

"Hum, well, I guess since she's the supervisor, you should not upstage her."

"I can't believe you are taking her side."

"Madison, get off your high horse, you have to learn to be submissive. And while we are on the subject, the bible even talks about wives submitting to their husbands.

I've invited some friends over on for a party on Saturday, cook something appetizing."

"Don't you think we should have discussed this before we have a party?"

"Nope. The end."

"What in the world is going on with you? Ever since I got here, you've changed."

"What's wrong with me?"

He turned around and glared at me. I got the feeling in the pit of my belly. The Lord said, look at his face, especially his eyes. What I saw was no soul. He looked like Satan himself.

"Forget it Drake; I don't feel like fighting. What time are they coming and how many did you invite?"

"Now that's more like it. About eight people will be here around six o'clock. Make sure the food is cooked on time. Try to do something with your hair and try to look presentable."

Ouch, that hair remark hurt.

The job itself was total confusion. Trying to unwind the contracts between the lawn care, phone system, office supplies and maintenance without prior knowledge was challenging. I was in Jamal's office several times because he had copies of the past contracts. Work on Friday was extremely difficult. Dealing with Linda while worrying about what's gotten into Drake. As usual, at dinner, I told Drake about my day. He stopped me in mid-sentence.

"So why are you in his office all of the time?" He said in an eerie soft voice.

"What are you talking about, he's the office manager and I work with him. I have to go in his office."

"Every time I call you Linda answers and tells me 'Yes, she's in Jamal's office again'. I don't want you in there anymore."

"Honey, you are being ridiculous, you know Linda dislikes me, and I have to work with Jamal."

I got the feeling in my belly, and the Holy Spirit said, look at his face.

Just then Drake jumped up from the table, took his massive arm and in one swoop, the entire dinner was on the floor.

"Drake, what is wrong with you? Why did you do that?"

"Don't call me ridiculous. As a matter of fact, don't ever talk back to me. I am the head of this house, and you will do what I say. Now get your black butt up and clean up this mess."

"You made the mess; you clean it up." I retorted.

"Oh no you didn't, you didn't just say that. Why, Maddie, why do you provoke me?"

"I am not provoking you. You need to chill out."

The Lord said, look at his face.

Then he said. "OK, it's on; I am going to beat you into submission. When I get through with you, you won't ever talk back to me."

He grabbed me by the throat and pinned me against the wall.

"Don't you try any of that Karate stuff either. Now, you repeat after me." He said while staring into my eyes.

"I will not talk back to my husband. I will not talk back to my husband. Say it."

"There is no way I'm saying that." I shouted while kicking and swinging at him.

His grip got tighter and tighter; I was about to lose consciousness. The next thing I know, I was laying on the floor, gagging for air holding my throat.

When I realized what happened, mad-mad Madison kicked in and I wanted revenge. The Lord said, there is a time to think and there is a time to feel. Now is the time to think even if you feel angry, do not react. I had to think my way out of this and get away from him before he kills me.

I ordered food for the Dinner party. Everyone had a nice time. Each person left after dinner except one couple.

The woman, Gail was a cute younger Italian lady. She wore a tight-fitting dress. Her perfume was too loud. I could smell her before I saw her.

Her husband was an older African American. He was on the couch, laid back with a big round gut and a balding head – a hole in his natural. In lovemaking, she had to get on top, because he would crush her.

"Madison, can I help you clean up the kitchen?" Gail asked

"Sure, I could use all the help I can get."

"So, how do you like your new house and the neighborhood?"

"Girl, I find it so charming. The major stores are within walking distance and the neighbors are nice."

"I know."

"Oh, do you live nearby or in Torrance?"

"No, we live in Hawthorne."

"So, how are you familiar with Torrance?"

"I thought Drake told you, he and I decorated your house?"

I could feel the blood boiling and crawling up my back. I was about to kill somebody in here. Then the small voice said

"Hold your peace; it's time to think and not feel."

"No, he didn't mention that. Thank you, you did a good job. How long did it take you to do all of this?"

"Not long, we worked almost every day for about three months. He told me what you liked and I shopped. Sometimes he went with me. Some people thought I was his wife." Then she laughs.

OK, now mad-mad Madison was plotting the getaway. I will not stand for this.

After the dishes, we went into the den to join the men.

"Honey, Ben has been telling me about their lifestyle." Drake said to me.

"What lifestyle?"

"Well, they are swingers. They want to swap partners."

"Man, have you lost your mind. You know our lifestyle, why would you even entertain an idea like that?"

"Don't knock it until you've tried it." Gail said with a smile and she looked at Drake.

I looked at Drake and he stops looking at Gail and looks at the floor.

I got the feeling in my belly. Something was not right here. This female has been in my house more than I have. This was her decorating style and now I believe she was having an affair with my husband.

Then the small voice said "Hold your peace; it's time to think and not feel."

"Well, Drake, let's discuss this in private and then you can get back with them."

"That sounds like our clue to leave." Ben said and stood up and stretched his 9 month pregnant sized gut falling over his pants.

We all hugged. I paid special attention to Drake and Gail. They knew I was watching.

While getting dressed for bed Drake brought up the swinging lifestyle.

"Babe, this could be the missing link in putting the passion back into our love life."

"Drake, I don't want another woman touching you, and I sure can't handle another man touching me."

"Come on honey, this could be fun. I could use something different."

"What has gotten into you, am I not enough? We can do something different to each other."

"OK, I guess you are not budging on the swinging lifestyle." He finally conceded.

"No, I am not."

"What do you think about a threesome?" "Man, will you give it a rest. No, I am not doing that either."

"Ok, I've got something you would enjoy. What if we did some S&M sex stuff?"

"I don't understand, what is that?"

"Trust me honey; you will enjoy it. I will blindfold you, and tie you to the bed and …."

"No. You will never. And I repeat never tie me to a bed or anything else."

"Baby, you have to get in the swing with the California lifestyle. Nobody's sex life is as boring as ours."

"Really Drake, and how would you know that?"

"I talk to people about things, and I know."

OK, I was going to test him.

"So if we did this threesome thing, who would be the third person?" I asked.

His eyes lit up like it was Christmas.

"I don't know, what about Gail?"

OK, Madison, think and not feel.

"Well honey, if I even thought about entertaining a threesome, I would want to have two men and just me. Who do you think the other man should be?"

Crickets. It was so quiet you could hear a mouse piss on cotton.

From that day on, Drake never brought up anything about an alternative sex lifestyle.

For the next few weeks, Drake was distant and quiet. He started putting his cell phone face down and on vibrate or completely off.

Being the analyst that I am, I went online to see his calling activity. Two numbers appeared multiple times every day. One was in Mexico.

"Who does he know in Mexico?"

I waited until I got to work and used a non-traceable secure line in the computer room and called the second number.

"Hello" Gail answers.

I decided to ask for myself.

"Yes, I am looking for Madison regarding the furniture recently purchased."

"Yes, this is she, how may I help you?"

I am thinking "The nerve of that whore."

I reply. "I was just verifying the phone number on our files for follow up. Thank you and have a wonderful day."

"Thank you, goodbye."

I was livid. It's time to think not feel. I waited a week, while Drake and I were having dinner and casual conversation.

"Hey, babe how was your day?" I asked in an upbeat tone.

"It was ok."

"You know, usually you talk about the places you and the staff go for lunch, what new restaurants have you tried lately?"

"Why do you want to know what I do on my lunch time? It's none of your business. Are you keeping tabs on me or what? Don't ever question me about my whereabouts. Get out of my face. Get up from this table right now and go to bed."

"I am not finished eating. I am not afraid of you. I will get up when I am ready."

Drake gave me a look, and the Lord said

"Look at his face."

When I really looked his face, into his eyes, he had no soul again and his features transformed into the face of a werewolf. It scared the poop out of me.

I got my happy behind up and washed the dishes. I was too frightened to get in bed with him, I slept on the couch.

After that Drake didn't come home or call for two days, I was frantic. I called his mother, the hospitals and his job, no one had seen him.

Finally, he came home.

"Drake, where have you been, I've been worried sick about you?"

"Haven't you learned yet, you don't ask the questions around here."

"I am your wife, it's about time you start acting like you're married. I am getting sick and tired of you treating me this way."

"You are sick and tired!" He shouted. "Let me show you how sick and tired I am of you. Your purpose in life is to take care of me. Your world revolves around me and what I need. I don't know why you don't understand that. I am going to beat some sense into your head. That's how sick and tired I am of you.

You know I've been to prison, what you don't know is I have two strikes. If I get a third one, it will not be for something minor, I am taking someone out with me."

He puts his face down and raises his eyes toward me.

The Lord said "look at his face."

I saw pure hate and my stomach was quivering. He started walking towards me taking long slow steps, stomping. The steps got shorter and faster. My God, he is running towards me.

I grabbed my purse and ran out the door no shoes and no jacket. I had to get away, I was petrified. My heart was beating hard, I am sure he heard it.

Why should I wait to get a beat down? I can't live like this. I was not raised this way. What did I do to make him hate me?

I went to a hotel. I opened my purse, and he had taken all of my cash. Luckily I hid my credit card in a different part of my purse. I called in sick the next day. I came to the house when I verified he was at work. I went through his desk. He was running a prostitution ring, two drug houses and he was writing coded messages to guys in Lompoc Prison. I kept digging, he had been locked up for drug dealing, assault, bank robbery, illegal selling weapons and attempted murder. This explains why a lot of the phone calls were to Mexico.

"My God, I've got to get out of here." I said while shaking in my boots.

He came to the house during the day when I was at work to change clothes, and I would be there at night while he worked. I was so terrified I threw up each night. I plotted my getaway. The weekend 2poc died, he went to Las Vegas for a fight. I called Judy who I met at church.

"I need your help."

"What is it Madison?"

"I have to leave Drake this weekend; can you help me pack up my things?"

"It is about time girl. I told you, your situation is not normal. This is the only choice you have. You must get out of there. Sure, I can help you. Do you need a truck or some men to help with the heavy stuff?"

"Yes, I need a truck and at least two men."

"Consider it done, what time do you want us there?"

"As soon as possible, he just left for Las Vegas with some chick."

"OK, give me a couple of hours, and we will be there."

I called the local U-Haul near the job for storage space.

A week ago I opened a PO Box near the job and had all of my mail transferred there.

Now I had to figure out where my dog and I were going to live.

"Light bulb moment… I remember the family reunion, and my distant cousin, Ms. Ada."

I still had her phone number.

"Hello, Ms. Ada?"

"Yes, who is this?" She said in a low frail voice.

"You might not remember me from the family reunion a few years ago, but I am Madison and I recently moved to California."

"Oh yes, I do remember you. Is everything alright honey?"

"No, it is not. I have left my husband and if I can't come live with you, I will have to go to a shelter. May I stay with you for a while until I find an apartment?"

"Come on baby."

My heart was light. I started crying tears of gratitude and relief.

Mad-mad Madison said you can't leave your house without leaving a calling card.

Drake was trying to impress this chick he took to Vegas, so he didn't take his CPAP Machine to control his sleep apnea. I pooped and peed in the water chamber and let it sit for an hour, then ran it through the tube. I rinsed it out and put it back on his side of the bed.

It was a long drive from Torrance to the San Fernando Valley.

After about 2 months, I found an apartment down the street from Ms. Ada. She became my bonus mother.

The Divorce was heart-wrenching. Drake showed up carrying a portable oxygen tank the size of a purse. He had lost weight. His attorney said he mysteriously developed an incurable repertory disease that requires oxygen 24/7. He brought his girlfriend, not Gail, to every meeting.

I had to fire my attorney because he had conversations with Drake and charged me.

My low life scum husband tried to get me to pay spousal support after 3 years of marriage. He wanted part of my pension, and he opened 5 charge cards with my name and charged them to the maximum. My credit report had twenty attempts at securing a loan in my name. The attorneys negotiated and came to the conclusion that either I pay off the charge cards, or he would get part of my pension for life. This was unfair. I opted to pay off HIS charge cards.

His attorney, my attorney, his parole officer and the judge each said don't ever let him know where you live because of his violent past criminal record.

The lesson learned from this failed marriage, he loved me until he got me away from my family, and then the real Drake came out. I looked up the word Narcissist: A person who uses excessive charm to woo and capture you and draw you into their world. When they know you love them and are dependent on them, they devalue, disrespect and sometimes become violent. This feeds their ego as they try to make up for the love and attention they didn't get as a child, especially from their mother. They are emotionally unavailable and not capable of giving or receiving true love. I had become Drakes Narcissist supply.

I finally told Jacob what happened.

"Hey Jacob, I have some news for you."

"Spit it out, I am busy."

"Drake and I are divorced, he was abusive towards me."

"Yes, I knew he was a rat. He did the same thing to one of Emily's friends who move here from out of town."

"What, you knew he was like this, and you didn't tell me."

"Well sis, I didn't want to get in your business."

"I wish you would have said something, this way I could have kept it in the back of my mind."

"Oh well, are you alright now?"

"Yes, I am fine. I'll talk to you later."

It took ten years to recover and look in the mirror and love myself. I didn't date. I didn't feel worthy of love. I felt like each person who saw me, saw the word loser on my forehead. Every time I looked in the mirror I saw an ugly person.

I learned to comb my hair and apply makeup without looking in the mirror. Drake told me I could never wear my blouse tucked in because I was trying to show off my butt. After 10 years, I finally felt comfortable tucking in my blouse.

I didn't feel comfortable telling my family and friends what Drake did to me. I went to a therapist to help sort out my feelings. It helped because I said the same thing over and over, and he had to listen.

I drowned myself in the bible, church and bible classes. I talked to God through the day. While shopping, I got looks like I was mentally challenged because I was talking to God out loud. I didn't care; I had God on spiritual speed dial and I was using it. It was such a comforting feeling going from being shattered and lost to being carefree.

In a bible study, we learned about Elizabeth. She was the mother of John the Baptist. When I joined my new church, I asked the members to call me by my middle name, Elizabeth. I had to put mad-mad Madison to rest.

SECOND CHANCE MARRIAGE

Carl lived down the street from my new house in West Covina, California.

He was a light-skinned, handsome Jamaican. When I walked past him, I heard an audible voice.

"He needs a friend." I looked around to see who was standing so close to me that they could whisper in my ear. No one was there. It had to be the Lord's sweet voice.

Since I didn't know anyone in my new neighborhood, we started talking when I walked the dog past his house. We talked for hours. He was a retired Architect. He showed me his designs, they were stunning, all over 10 million dollar projects.

There were three houses between ours. We would walk to each other's house to visit. We watched the ball games and had expressive conversations about politics, religion, family and sports. I was not romantically attracted to him because I was done with the love thing.

But it was nice having a friend living close for conversation and company.

One night I cooked and invited him over to watch a game after dinner.

"You sit there; I will put the dishes in the sink for you." He said with a smile.

"Thank you, that's nice of you."

"I always like a nice glass of ice water after dinner; can I get you some water?"

I was thinking "What the heck, this was exactly what my dad did for my mother; I don't remember telling him that."

"Yes, I would"

As he sat the glass down, he looked at me and said "Delicious, you put your foot in it, girl. Thank you for taking the time to prepare it for me."

"No problem, I had to eat anyway." I said trying not to be too shocked because my dad said that to my mom after every dinner.

Over the next two years, we got closer as friends; we went everywhere together and shared everything. His friends became my friends. We went dancing together; he joined my church. I was delighted with this arrangement. In a Laker's halftime game he tried to kiss me.

"What are you doing?" I screeched.

"Woman, I have been in love with you since I met you two years ago. Elizabeth, I watched you walk your dog every day for a month until I got the nerve to say something. Then you stopped walking the dog, and I waited another month for you to walk by. I didn't want to stalk you, but I had to get to know you."

"Oh no, Carl, I can't do this. Please don't destroy a great friendship."

"Since we started as friends, I understand you, and I love you for who you are and will never hurt you like those in your past. I know for sure I will marry you."

"Keep it. I've heard that love Bull before. Please leave my house!"

He left with his head down and dragging his feet. He reminded me of a puppy with its tail tucked between its legs.

That night I got on my knees. "Lord, I don't want to become involved, it hurts too much. If I am supposed to fall in love and marry Carl, please make it clear to me. I don't know how to do this love thing. I have failed many times and can't get it right. Daddy, deep down inside, I trust Carl and he is truly my best friend. I want to give him a chance at love, but I am too afraid. I've trusted in the past and was wrong. I don't want mad-mad Madison to come out and kill him with my sharp mouth. Daddy, please help me figure this out. I put this in your hands. In your Son Jesus name I pray."

The next day Carl showed up unannounced.

"What are you doing here?"

"I have come to make you my wife."

"Man, if you don't get out of here with that nonsense, I will throw you out."

"Come on Elizabeth; let me take you to dinner."

"Now you're talking, let's go to the Thai Restaurant on Nogales Street, across from the high school."

"Yes, I know, that's our spot."

When we got there, it was empty, which was unusual.

A string orchestra came from the kitchen playing softly, followed by my brother Jacob, the three musketeers, my mother, Ms. Ada, my friends from the church and all of our mutual friends.

"What's going on Carl?" I questioned with a wrinkled forehead.

I looked around, and he was on one knee holding the ring I saw in the Diamond District in Downtown Los Angeles. It was beautiful pink halo diamond surrounded by white diamonds.

"Will you marry me, Madison Elizabeth?" He announced.

"Oh, how could I say no?"

He slipped the ring on my finger.

"A perfect fit." I said.

"Yes, we are." He said. And we embraced.

We had a celebration at the restaurant. I was ecstatic.

For two days it was such a pleasure having the family with me. I enjoyed long talks with my mother. Jacob was unusually easy to be around. The kids were well behaved. I got to know their personalities. Everyone I loved was near me. It was such an overwhelming feeling of peace that filled my house. Before going to bed, I got on my knees. I had a talk with God.

"Thank you, Daddy, for making me whole again. I will always give you the praise and recognition. Finally, you sent someone who gets me and loves me. He does not do things to piss me off, and I am always calm when I was with him.

Thank you, Lord for restoring my faith in men and making me realize I had to wait and go through this dry season while you were preparing Carl for me and me for him.

Now, Lord, I can exhale. I have my permanent calm in you first Daddy and then Carl who maintains me. Thank you, I can slow down and enjoy a new life with him.

I can finally take off my body shaper. I can see in his eyes he cherishes me and considers me a priority and not an afterthought. I am his queen. I will follow him as he follows you.

What is most important, he loves you Lord. All praises to you my God. You are the great I AM, the Prince of Peace, the Almighty God and the only one who could soften my heart. Lord, for the first time in many years, I am truly happy and content. Thank you, Lord. My heart is about to burst with the gratitude and love. In your son's Jesus name I pray amen."

The wedding was set for Valentine's Day. We sent out heart shaped wedding invitations. It is, of course, a Valentine's theme. We are both excited. The colors were Black and White, with red accents. All arrangements are made; photographer, videographer, flowers, minister, church, reception hall, and honeymoon. We are just waiting for the day. Jacob wanted to walk me down the aisle, but I told him I wanted to walk alone because my Daddy (God) is walking with me down the aisle.

On December 24 at 3 pm, Carl had a massive stroke and died. I could not understand why God would bring his man into my life, allow me to experience real true love and nurturing from a man other than my dad; and then take him from me.

I was in a daze. I didn't know what to do. I couldn't feel anything. While in the middle of planning my wedding, I had to stop. How was I going to plan a funeral, cremation and send his ashes to New York to his family? Where do I begin?

Needless to say, God and I were not on speaking terms for a while.

Everywhere I went I was reminded of Carl; Our restaurant, our dance place, our grocery store, our park, our movie theater. A commercial came on that we joked about, and I cried for 3 hours.

I surrounded myself with the many little things he purchased for no reason at all, just because he saw it and it reminded him of me.

I missed him so much. There was part of me that will never recover. I understand why they say when someone dies; they take a part of you with them. I wore his shirts to smell him. Oh my God! This pain was like nothing I've ever felt. It was a low, dull, throat growling moan in the pit of my stomach that makes my shoulders curl forward and slowly bends my entire body over and downward. I was an empty shell. This man loved me, and I made me feel pretty and validated.

"Oh God why?"

Lesson Learned from Carl: I was worthy of being loved. However God has the last word. I don't understand God right now, but I trust Him.

DRAFT

BACK TO THE ROOTS

After a few years, I moved back to Detroit. I needed my family. Jacob and the triplets, Kimberly, Kayla, and Cameron (three musketeers) were helpful and attentive.

I was on a flexible work schedule. I arranged my schedule in order to drive the three musketeers to and from school. I enjoy their stories and they keep me updated on the latest songs and dances.

"Auntie, my teacher saw you and asked me if you were married." Kimberly said.

"And what did you tell him?"

"I told him you were not married."

"That's enough. I don't want to be bothered."

"But Auntie, he is a nice guy and he wants your phone number."

"No way, we are done talking about this." I shut her down.

One day, I got a call from the school; Kimberly was sick and they requested me to pick her up. I drove like I was shot out of a cannon to get to the school. I'm wondering if she has the flu, or was she injured, or God knows what.

I checked in with security and rushed to the office.

There was my baby all sick with vomit on her cute little dress.

"Come here baby, give Auntie a hug. I will take care of you."

I felt her forehead and neck; she was as hot as the oven. She was sweating like someone turned on a faucet on her body. I called Emily to get the doctor's name and number.

"Girl, Kimberly is sick, where should I take her?"

"She ain't sick; she just doesn't want to stay in school."

"I am telling you, the girl is sick, she is hot and has thrown up her breakfast."

"OK, in that case, take her to Children's hospital in the Detroit Medical Center and I will meet you in the ER."

Jacob picked up Kayla and Cameron and brought them to the hospital. Kimberly had Pneumonia and had to be put on a respirator. It was touch and go for three days, but prayer changes things.

Each night, one of us stayed at the hospital. One evening, three of her teachers visited.

"Hello Aunt Elizabeth, Kimberly has told me all about you, my name is Ray."

"You must be her teacher she wanted me to meet. I'm pleased to meet you Ray."

"If there is anything you need, please do not hesitate to contact me." He said as he squeezed my hand.

"OK, we will reach you at the school."

Just then, one of the female teachers came over to introduce herself and claim her territory; Ray.

"I am Kimberly's history teacher and this young lady is her Gym teacher."

"Hi ladies, we all are thankful you came to check on Kimberly, your visit means the world to us."

The history teacher grabs Ray's arm and the group leaves.

The next day Ray calls the hospital room and I answer.

"I am sorry we had to leave early, how is Kimberly doing?" He asks.

"She is coming along fine, she will be released tomorrow."

"Excellent. Elizabeth, would you mind if we went out for drinks after work?"

"Actually I would mind, it appears you have a relationship with the history teacher and I am not about to be a side chick. You can take the drinks and shove them."

"Oh, hold on its just drinks. I was not asking you to have my baby. Forget it. You sound like you have some serious issues Psycho Chick."

"Maybe I do have issues but its men like you who created me. Don't approach my niece about me again or you will see the real Psycho Chick."

I hung up.

"I got rid of that male whore. I am too old and tired for games."

CHICAGO

I went to Chicago for a surprise 25th wedding anniversary of my cousin and her husband. I was the MC. I think I am funny, but others think I am corny which makes me the perfect MC. It was a double celebration for me because I just received my MBA. I didn't mention it because this was their day.

Their best friend James drove in from Detroit also. We met a few times, and he was a pretty cool guy. After the celebration, we talked.

"Hey Madison, how is Detroit treating you?"

"Very well James. I am going by my middle name of Elizabeth."

"Oh, why did you change?"

"I would like to take on the personality and faith of Elizabeth, the mother of John the Baptist. When I hear the name, I am reminded I am important to God."

"Wow, that's pretty deep, Elizabeth." Do you want to go out for coffee tonight after the celebration?"

"No,"

I was not wearing my body shaper. A girl has to be careful.

"When are you going back to Detroit?"

"We are leaving tomorrow afternoon."

"Here take my card and call me when you get back, I want to catch with you."

"OK." I wait a few weeks and decided to call James.

"Hello."

"Hello James, this is Elizabeth, how are you?"

"I am fine; it's about time you called. I have been waiting by the phone and checking my voice mail, hoping I didn't miss your call."

I could hear females in the background.

"Did I catch you at an inconvenient time? It sounds like you have company."

"No, I am glad you called. I have a few friends over. Wait a minute; let me go to another room where I can have some privacy. Ms. Elizabeth, tell me something good."

"James, I don't know anything good, I just thought I would call to say hi. I can see you are busy, I'll talk to you later, bye."

I hung up. I didn't wait for him to say bye. It sounded like he was having a party at 3:30 in the afternoon. Who does that? Based on what I heard, he was a baller. If he calls I won't be surprised, if he does not call, I won't be disappointed.

At 11:00 pm James calls.

"Hello Elizabeth"

"Man, are you crazy, it's too late to be calling people. I was asleep; don't call me this late again. Boy bye."

The next day at about 3:30 pm he calls again.

"Hello Elizabeth, I hope this is a better time to call you."

"Yes it is James, I apologize for going off on you last night, but I need my rest."

"No apology necessary, you were justified. You can be sure I won't call you that late again."

We laughed.

"Can I take you for coffee and we can get caught up in each other's lives?"

"How about now?" I said and to catch him off guard.

"Well, ok, give me a few minutes."

"James, meet me at the coffee place in the RenCen at 5:00."

"Just take over Ms. Elizabeth. I like a girl who knows what she wants. You got it, I will see you there."

"Ok, bye."

I had to get myself together. I want to look cute, but not thirsty. I don't want anything too tight on the top or bottom. But, for sure, I was wearing my warden of my Garden of Eden.

I looked cute in my Black jeans, black and white knit blouse, black and white earrings and a black choker and five-inch hills. The jeans are a little snug, but that's life. A little dab of perfume and I was off. I was purposely ten minutes late. I wanted to make an entrance and make him look for me.

"Good afternoon beautiful." He says flashing his smile.

"Hello James, how are you?" And I extend my hand for a firm handshake.

"Wow woman, don't be so cold and loosen up. Remember, we go back a long way. I have known you since Ned was a pup."

"So what do you mean loosen up? I am not cold. All I said was Hello James."

"I see an attractive woman with a chip on her shoulder the size of this building. I am not your enemy. I am just trying to reconnect with you. Girl, what has happened to you? This is not the Elizabeth I once knew."

"Nothing has happened to me, I am just too tired for games and I don't have the patience to wade through the bull."

"I believe the girl I once knew and adored is in there somewhere. But you are coming across like a bitter and mean woman.

Maybe you are not having a good day, or something I don't know. But what I do know and what appears crystal clear is there are some unresolved issues with you. If you will trust me, I can help you walk through them. "

"You will help me? Boy Bye. Where do you come off telling me that you see I have issues? I'll bet you have issues too. Let's talk about your issues, shall we? Trust me Part'na ; you don't want to piss me off. Do you think you're a therapist or something?"

"Actually I am one of the most popular therapists next to those on TV.

We laugh.

"I like watching the TV shrinks." I said.

"Whatever, babe, my point is I am an excellent listener and a better friend. Elizabeth, please talk to me."

"I'm not your babe. Sure we can talk. You first. Trust is earned, not given."

"No problem. I don't know if your cousin told you, but I am a father. Yep, I have a 5 year old daughter. I did not marry her mother, but we remain friends for my little princess Olivia. She is my world, and I will do anything for her. Her mom, Terra, brings her to me on the weekends we do fun stuff together."

I listened to every word, and watch his body language as he talks about his child and her mother.

"It is nice that you and her mom remained friends. Do you have a picture of Olivia?"

"A picture, shoot girl, I have a phone full of pictures."

He quickly pulls out his phone and instantly brings up pictures.

"Bam, look at my baby."

"Awww She is cute." I genuinely mean it. She was a caramel color brown, with cute twisted pigtails with bows on each one. Her glasses are oversized for her face. Her most recent pictures show her two front teeth missing.

"Yes, she is. I know I will have a difficult time when it is time for her to date. I hate to think about it. Enough about my baby, let's get back to our conversation. My patients are millennials or in people in their late 40's and early 50's. I enjoy sports, in particular, Basketball. My basement has lots of Detroit Pistons memorabilia. Sometimes the team disappoints me, but they are still my home team. I enjoy music. My favorite group of all times is the original old school Temptations; I like the first group, not the remixed one. Its old school, but those guys not only could sing but could outperform anybody."

"It seems we have similar taste in music and sports. What about your family?" I asked.

"I have two sisters and one brother. They live in different states, and I do miss the family bonding thing. My parents didn't stay together, but they never divorced.

My dad was not nice to my mother. He ran around on her and caused her to become nasty and unkind. He died about two years ago. He had another set of children we discovered at his funeral. I could not believe the grief my mother felt for someone who treated her poorly."

James took a deep breath and said.

"Enough about me tell me what's been going on with you."

"Well, I am not an exciting person. I never had children. I am still working for Ford Motor Company as an E-Business Analyst. My passions are ballroom and line dancing. I talk to God on a regular basis. I go to church, but I am in the Bench Member Ministry."

We both laugh.

I say "Look at the time, it's almost 10:00 pm. I need to go."

"Oh yes, we both know how important your sleep is to you. I would still like to get to know you better. May I call you tomorrow?"

"Yes, I would like that."

As I stood up, he helped me with my jacket. He walked me to the car. I was hoping he did not try to kiss me or anything. He gave me a hug and watched me pull off before he walked to his car.

For a year, James called every morning and every evening. He enjoyed hearing about my day, and I liked listening to him talk about his.

I have always lived on the east side of Detroit. James lived in Rosedale Park which was on the west side. Sometimes it's like going to a different country, but it's actually only a 30-minute drive.

Since the housing market was down, prices in the better neighborhoods were low. I found a house for sale on the west side that was in foreclosure. It was in the Palmer Park area. It was unusual to find a nice ranch house in the middle of all of these mini mansions.

James was helpful while moving. Mon didn't like me moving on the west side. She was content with my promised to visit her at least once a week.

After a few months of moving on the west, James started to change. Every Thursday night after 7:00 PM he could not be found. I became leery about him ghosting on Thursday nights.

"Good morning baby, how did you sleep?" He said opening his usual morning call.

"Good morning to you too! Yes, I slept well. James, I am curious, why didn't you answer your phone last night when I called?"

"The phone must have been on the charger, and I forgot to take it off of vibrate when I went to bed."

"That seems to be the case every Thursday night. Now, what's going on with you on Thursday nights?"

"Hold up Elizabeth. Are you trying to accuse me of something?"

"If the shoe fits?"

"Baby, I can't believe you are accusing me of something just because I didn't answer the phone."

"Well, believe it. Do you have a side chick who is settling for one day out of the week?"

"Calm down babe; you are tripping over nothing."

"Since when did you ever call me babe. In case you forgot, I am baby or honey. Babe must be your Thursday night side chick. And don't ever tell me to calm down. I will say what I want to say, how I want to say it and when I want to say it. Calm down. Please don't insult me. You better believe you don't want to piss me off. Now James, answer the question: What is going on every Thursday night?"

"No, I will not be interrogated because of a missed call."

"James it's not just a missed call, it's a missed call every Thursday night." I screamed. I hear myself, but I can't stop yelling at him. "James, I will not be played. You should know me by now."

"Listen Elizabeth, why don't I call you later and we will talk about this."

"Naw to the naw, we will finish this right now."

"I must get ready for work, we will talk later, bye." He said and hung up the phone.

"Oh no, he didn't just hang up on me." I said while looking at the phone.

I called right back. "No, no, no; he didn't just send me straight to voice mail on his cell phone?" I was fuming.

"Oh James, you want to play games. You better call me back right now." I screamed my voice mail message into the phone.

I waited five minutes, no call, ten minutes, and no call. I felt my blood boiling, and I was coming unglued.

"This was war."

I called his cell phone twenty times in one hour but did not leave a message.

I texted him and waited for a reply. No reply for two hours.

I felt like the chick in that movie, "I will not be ignored."

Finally, after work, I got a text from James:

"Elizabeth, you have shown me a side of you I simply cannot wrap my head around. Based on your reaction, I can no longer be in this relationship. I wish you well."

I was devastated. "Was he breaking up with me in a text?"

"That punk chicken. He does not have the balls to face me in person about his Thursday night side chick."

I texted him back.

"James, if that's the way you want to end this two-year relationship, then you are a bigger coward than I thought. But, we are not done until I say we are done."

It was about 10:00 pm and time for bed. I got on my knees and prayed to God.

"Lord, I believe I have made a terrible mistake. As you know, I do appreciate James, but I allowed myself to get carried away with my temper. I could not contain mad-mad Madison, and I said some terrible things.

Daddy, I need your comfort for the stupid mistake I made. I believe James has been faithful to me. I let my imagination get the best of me regarding his location on Thursday nights. Lord, help me. I need you to stabilize my mind and keep me focused and calm.

Lord, please forgive me for only talking to you when I am in trouble. Please forgive me for using you like a combat shelter, only when I need cover. Please forgive me for not including you in all of my big and little decisions during every day. Daddy, my heart aches because I believe I have lost James. Give me some peace. I want to sleep and be ready for the challenges the day will bring. In your son Jesus I pray, Amen."

After I dried my eyes, I slept well. In the morning, I was waiting for my morning call from James. No phone call and no text.

"Dear God, I beg you, please help me."

I did my daily routine like a robot, dressing for work, driving to work and working. I decided to catch lunch alone at the Soul Food Restaurant in Southfield. Low and behold, there was James and his coworkers.

James saw me enter. He got up and walked cautiously toward me. I got nervous. Was he going to cuss me out, confront me or what?

"Hey baby, we both said and did some things that were not cool yesterday. I would like a chance to begin again." He says flashing his Billy D. smile.

"Yes, I would like too also."

"Great! I was just finishing lunch with my coworkers. Honey, you are stunning. I thought an angel walked through the doors. The dress accents your well-toned body. I just want to take you in my arms right now." He said and kissed me on my neck.

"Is it alright if I come by your house tonight around 6:00 PM?"

"Works for me." I said with a smile.

He bends down and kisses me on my cheek, and says "I will see you later gorgeous."

He gets the waitress attention and then says, "Please put her bill on my tab."

I waited for James to come. It was 6:00 pm, and he was never late. Then he calls. "Baby, I am on the way, there was a lot of traffic out here."

"Ok James, don't have me waiting a long time. Now, how much longer do you think you will be?"

"Madison, I'm on the way. Maybe about thirty minutes, give or take a few."

"OK, I am not waiting much longer than 6:30."

I had to let him know I was hip to that old calling game.

I hung up the phone and prayed.

"Dear Lord, please keep me calm and keep mad-mad Madison under control."

At 6:15 James rings the doorbell. He was standing there with flowers and a huge smile.

"Get in here man. This has been a long day of missing you."

We kiss.

James explained in great detail about Thursday nights.

"Elizabeth, please don't talk, just listen. I have to level with you Elizabeth. First of all, I was wrong for sending a break up text when I should have said that in person.

Secondly, I was wrong for letting you think you were imagining me ghosting on Thursday nights. OK, Honey here is the big one.

I have a friend who was dying of stage four pancreatic cancer. It's a female, who does not have any family. A group of friends have decided to take care of her. As a matter of fact, the first time you called, the group was here discussing her care.

My day in the rotation was Thursday from 7:00 PM until 2:00 AM. Yes, I do ghost, but for a noble reason.

Elizabeth, don't get upset, this person is the mother of my child. Her name is Terra. I didn't want to tell you because I knew you would fly off the handle. Please understand I have to do this and know with every fiber in your body that I love only you.

Honey, she does not have a romantic place in my heart, it all belongs to you. I have an obligation to do my part. I hope you understand." He says.

"Whew, information overload. No, I don't like it that you tried to twist it around to make me think I was crazy and imagining things.

I do appreciate you telling me the truth. James, I trust you. Please forgive me for accusing you of a side chick. I am sorry I blew up your phone with text messages and voice mail messages."

"Elizabeth, that was a bit extreme. I must admit, it frightened me because I thought you had gone full-throttle psycho on me. I thought you would slash my tires or take a baseball bat to my windshield.

Because of my training, and I know what you have gone through, it does not take much to push you over the edge. You go to this warped reasoning as your defense mechanism protecting yourself.This behavior acts as your buffer cushioning the blow to avoid getting hurt again. I understand why you resort to this distorted line of thinking."

We both laugh.

For the next six months, James kept me informed about Terra; her treatments, sickness and remission. I became accustomed to not hearing from him on Thursday evenings. I told him about the natural cures my mom used and others I read about on the Internet especially Dr. Sabi.

In one year, Terra was cured. The cancer was gone. She went back to work and bought a new Green Ford Escape.

Life was wonderful. James and I are back on schedule. Terra no longer needs 24/7 care. Mom was healthy, and the three musketeers are coming over this weekend. Jacob was starting to act like a caring father. Life was beautiful.

THE DAY TRAFFIC DETOURED

Why, did the traffic have to detour past James House that day?

Now here I go to see the judge after shooting two people.

"Madison Elizabeth Canter how do you plead?" The judge asked with a stern voice.

"Your honor, I am guilty, sorry and remorseful."

"You will be sentenced in two weeks. Officers, take her away."

I glanced at my mother. I could see the pain and disappointment on her face. Jacob would not look at me.

In a week, I got a visitor. It was James.

"Oh, my God, I am glad I didn't kill you." I said with enthusiasm.

"You tried, but as you can see I survived, and so did my cousin."

"Your cousin?"

"Yes, my cousin Mariam was visiting from Chicago and she has the same kind of vehicle as Terra. I know you thought Terra was at my house that night.

I tried to explain this to you before you started shooting. Girl, you have got to get your temper under control. Being locked up may be the best thing for you."

He continues, "I just wanted you to know this before your sentencing next week. I am not pressing charges."

"Thank you James. I don't know what to say except I am sorry." I said and started to cry.

"Baby, you have to be strong in here, never show any weakness or they will take advantage of you. It's a new life for you now, learn to adjust.

Another thing, I know we've dated for a few years. The thought of losing me brought Terra and I closer. We are back together raising our daughter Olivia. We are going to be a family. I will marry her in a few months. I hope we can still be friends when you get out." He says with a smile.

"What! I thought we were a couple. We did so much together."

"I know Elizabeth; I mislead you while keeping the door open to Terra. I was trying to figure out what I wanted. Please forgive me. I brought you a gift; it's a book 'Discerning the Voice of God." He says as he nervously extends his shaking hand holding the book.

"I know you pray to God, but I'm not sure if you stop to listen to what God is telling you. This book will help you listen to, and follow God's voice and not the Devil."

DRAFT

LISTENING TO GOD

That night I prayed in silent to God. I didn't want the inmates to think I was soft.

"Lord, I know I am a major league screw up, and I am sorry. You've heard it all before from me, and I can't make any promises that I will do better. Daddy, I am asking you to open my heart and my mind as I read this book James gave me.

I want to hear your voice and follow only you. Lord, create in me a clean heart so when you come into my heart I can feel you and obey only you. Lord, I repent of all of my sins and I understand repentance is to admit it and then quit it.

Daddy, I am in your hands. By the way, I know there are consequences for me shooting James and his cousin, but will you soften the heart of the judge. Thank you, in your son Jesus name I pray. Amen."

After the prayer, I sat still for a while and felt a little quiver in my stomach. I believe that was the Lord giving me peace about my situation.

The judge sentences me to five years' probation because I didn't have a record and I didn't kill anyone. I can no longer own a gun.

My prayers are working. I was only listening to God's voice. Mad-mad Madison has been put to rest. The test will be when someone pisses me off and I hear Gods calming voice.

It was part of my self-therapy every morning I ask the Lord to amplify my spiritual senses. I want those 5 senses to help me hear and distinguish His voice. I will be quiet, listen and then feel the presence of God.

I contacted every person I had done wrong. When I think about my smart mouth and the things I did, I was so remorseful that it hurts in the pit of my stomach.

I apologized from my heart and asked for their forgiveness. If I caused financial misfortune, I offered to correct it. I shared the Love of the Lord with each person. I explain that the Lord was working on me and I will do better. I know the Lord was pleased with me, I can feel it down in my soul and I get a little quiver in my stomach.

I was giving back to the community by working with the local food bank. I was working with the Hospitality Ministry at the church. I loved greeting everyone as they came into the house of worship.

I realize one is a whole number and a man does not make or break me. I will seek the Lord and he will give me the desires of my heart, not necessarily an earthly companion. I have been blessed with the important things we cannot touch with our hands but with our hearts; love, peace, understanding and kindness. I was praying for wisdom to make me a better servant of the Lord. I have all of the desires of my heart.

While driving on I-94 coming from church on Sunday, my radio was on blast while listing to the 24-hour gospel station. The car behind me was traveling at a high rate of speed. All of a sudden a car comes across two lanes in an attempt to exit.

"Oh no, I can't stop."

I hit a brick or something on the Freeway. The right side of the car went up first then my whole car went airborne, and I could not control it.

I heard glass breaking as the car tumbled and rolled sideways down the freeway. My head was hitting the steering wheel and the window. I was bouncing around. The airbag opened and snapped my head back. There was blood on the airbag from my head.

The car stopped rolling when it slammed into the brick wall. Finally quiet from all of the rolling and jarring of my body. I was hanging upside down. I felt warm blood rolling from my head and legs; however, I was not in pain.

"Dear Lord, please don't let me die." I said in a whispered voice.

I heard cars skidding and what sounded like car doors slamming. There were people screaming at me asking if I am OK. I tried to answer, but could not respond.

There was a young guy standing near the car, looking at me with a closed mouth smile. His calmness stuck out and separated him from the others running and screaming. He reached in and removed me from the car.

He said, "It's time to go."

"Go where? We have to wait for the police." I told him.

He smiled and said;

"Madison, God is waiting for you. Never again will you ever feel pain of any kind from anyone. You have finished your race. You have learned your lessons. It is time for you to go and claim your rewards for a job well done."

I turned from the angel and looked at the car. I saw my body damaged and bleeding. My neck was broken, and my head was in an awkward position. My right leg was severed and bleeding like a faucet. The good Samaritans trying to help are frantic. Now, their voices are in whispered tones.

I turn to my angel and say, "Does God want to take me now before I have time to mess up again?"

He gently took my hand and we slowly ascended into the clouds. I was as light as a feather. My heart was leading me up. I don't have to breathe. I was fully aware of what is going on. My new celestial body is exquisite. I am semi-transparent with a light blue glow. My wings are totally transparent with a design similar to the design on a fly's wings with a slight blue hue. Instinctively, my wings are propelling me up.

There is a calm light breeze. There is a sweet fragrance of eucalyptus. A muted light eliminates one cloud. As the cloud opens, there is the aroma of sandalwood. An army of people are gliding gracefully towards me. Leading the army are my dad and Carl. In the distance, I can see my Daddy sitting on his throne beckoning for me to come to him. My heart is satisfied. I behold Him face to face. I am finally home sitting at Jesus' feet.

THE END

Made in the USA
Middletown, DE
21 May 2018